At that moment, two ⬚⬚⬚⬚⬚⬚⬚⬚⬚⬚⬚⬚⬚⬚⬚⬚⬚⬚⬚⬚⬚ er
they merged into a single ⬚⬚⬚⬚⬚⬚⬚⬚⬚⬚⬚⬚⬚⬚, the pair of
hardcases ran toward the rill. Halting on top, they stared into
the valley. It was apparent even to Silkin, who was more brutal
than intelligent, that their company had failed in the duty to
which they had been assigned.

"Holy Mother!" Silkin said. "They've sure busted up that
son of a bitch. It's lucky for us Moe Buller's gone to Washington."

"It'd be easier was he here," Packard corrected him.

"How'd you mean, 'easier,' Pack?" Silkin asked.

"Moe's not going to take it kind that the bridge's been
blowed up, 'specially with his brother running things when it
happened," the sergeant major explained. "And, knowing him
like I do, he'll be looking for somebody else to take the blame.
So we'll give him Cogshill."

"Cogshill?" repeated the corporal, face blank with incomprehension.

"Nobody else but," Packard affirmed. "Leave *me* do the
talking and back up everything I say. Handled right, Silky,
there's money in this for you and me."

Books by J. T. Edson

THE NIGHT HAWK
NO FINGER ON THE TRIGGER
THE BAD BUNCH
SLIP GUN
TROUBLED RANGE
THE FASTEST GUN IN TEXAS
THE HIDE AND TALLOW MEN
THE JUSTICE OF COMPANY Z
McGRAW'S INHERITANCE
RAPIDO CLINT
COMANCHE

A Matter of Honor

J. T. EDSON

A DELL BOOK

Published by
Dell Publishing
a division of
Bantam Doubleday Dell Publishing Group, Inc.
666 Fifth Avenue
New York, New York 10103

ISBN: 0-440-20936-6

Printed in the United States of America

Published simultaneously in Canada

July 1991

10 9 8 7 6 5 4 3 2 1

RAD

For Eve and Ed Harris of "San Jacinto"
Best wishes, you-all

Prologue

Lightning was flashing intermittently and, deeply menacing, thunder was rumbling somewhere far to the southwest.

However, while clouds were scudding across the sky over Washington, D.C., and were occasionally obscuring the full moon, as yet the inclement weather was having no other effect. There were, in fact, moments of brilliant illumination when the room reappeared from behind its temporary concealment. In spite of this (possibly because of the suggestion that the distant heavy storm might be approaching), there seemed to be an atmosphere of brooding over the capital city of a United States of America that was now divided against itself.

It was, all in all, the kind of night that conveyed an impression of exuding a distinct aura of impending evil.

Although gutted by fire after the city had fallen into the hands of the British army in 1814, to such an extent that only the walls were left standing, the Executive Mansion—to give the correct name to the official residence of the President—had

been rebuilt, refurnished, and had had its exterior painted in
the fashion that produced the more generally employed name,
"the White House." Built between 1791 and 1799 from designs
by James Hoban, who had followed closely the plans of the
"seats" of the dukes of Leinster, near Dublin, Eire, the two-
story building of Virginia freestone was a simple structure with
its principal exterior ornaments being an Ionic portico and bal-
ustrade.

Restlessly pacing the floor of his private study, the present
incumbent of the White House thought the distant threat of the
storm was in keeping with his mood.

Tall, gaunt, bearded, and somberly clad, Abraham Lincoln,
sixteenth President of the United States, has become so familiar
via numerous sketches and caricatures in the newspapers of the
day as to require no further description. There was, nevertheless, something of the essence of his greatness in his appearance
which required no fine raiment to enhance it. It was in evidence
even though, being in the seclusion and privacy he desired that
night, he was wearing only a collarless white shirt and black
trousers, drawing solace from walking barefoot—as he had, of
necessity, so often done during his far from affluent early life—
he had discarded his boots and socks.

Pausing by a window, its drapes left open regardless of numerous warnings from various people responsible for his safety
that to do so offered opportunities for intended assassins, the
President looked out to see whether the storm was in fact coming closer. Coinciding with a clear period of the full moon, he
had a good view of his immediate surroundings. Not for the
first time, he wished Major Pierre Charles L'Enfant and An-
drew Ellicott had placed the White House and Capitol nearer
together when laying out the plans for the city in the late 1780s.
No work on the construction of the latter would be taking
place, the time being seven-thirty on a Saturday evening, but he
always enjoyed looking at it and envisaging how it was to be
upon completion. Despite voluble complaints about the cost
from some quarters, he considered he was stating unequivocally
his unshaken faith in the Union and the capital city by insisting

that the erection of the dome be continued. Yet the pleasure with which he regarded the sight of the work being carried out was lessened by the thought of why the suggestions for economies had been made. He hated to be reminded, even indirectly, of the measures currently being found necessary to preserve the Union for which the Capitol was to be the symbol.

Although Abraham Lincoln had no doubt history would give him credit—or the blame, dependent upon the point of view of the writer—for the decision to fight against those states wishing to secede from the Union, such had never been his wish. If he could have maintained the Union by declaring opposition to the very vocal antislavery lobby, he would have done so and sought to bring about emancipation by verbal persuasion. However, he had known that to do so would merely delay the almost inevitable clash between the chiefly industrialized northern free states and the mainly agricultural southern slave states. There were powerful factions on both sides of the Mason-Dixon line committed to open conflict. He was all too aware that, despite offering a more readily understood reason to the poorer sections of the white community in the North—who would be required to bear the brunt of the fighting should war come—slavery was neither the only nor the most important issue causing the dissension. Therefore, even if the attack by Confederate forces upon Fort Sumter had not supplied the metaphorical match to touch off the explosion,[1] some other incident would have served to supply the excuse for a declaration of war. Nor could the moderate groups on either side have averted the unavoidable result.

Now, throughout much of the vast land, opposing armies and smaller forces were locked in mortal combat. Warships flying the Stars and Stripes or Stars and Bars (flags of the United and Confederate States) sought for and destroyed the merchant vessels of the other side upon the high seas. Already the latter were wreaking havoc upon the whaling fleet of the

1. The attack took place on April 14, 1861, Fort Sumter being in the harbor of Charleston, South Carolina. J. T. E.

former that would take many years to put to rights when peace finally came.

In many ways, happening in an era and a country devoted to the search for technological progress, the conflict had developed into the first of the modern "total" wars. For all that, at least where members of the regular army and navy were concerned, the age-old conventions governing the behavior of fighting men were upheld. If a truce was granted, or parole given and accepted, in general the terms were adhered to.[2] However, as is always the case—human nature being what it is—much of the technological development was devoted to improving methods of killing.

Self-contained metallic cartridges were already paving the way for repeating rifles to become practical and allowed simple forms of machine guns to make their appearance.[3] Warfare had taken to the air, if not yet in actual combat, with the use of observation balloons.[4] Albeit by "submersibles" rather than true "submarines," with one notable exception, fighting was going on beneath the surface of the sea.[5] Refinement in high-explosive shells, sometimes filled with incendiary compounds to increase their effect, and employed in sieges, spelled the first stages of the end for massive man-made fortresses. Throwing corpses down wells that would be used by the enemy explored, without any full understanding of its ramifications, the horrors

2. What happened when a parole was given, accepted and broken is described in: Part Two, *"A Convention of War,"* Under the Stars and Bars. J. T. E.

3. An example of an early form of machine gun is given in: *The Devil Gun.* J. T. E.

4. An incident involving the use of an observation balloon is described in: *The Big Gun.* J. T. E.

5. The exception was the *Hunley* of the Confederate States' Navy. Although its motive power was supplied by eight men who operated cranks to turn the propellor, the vessel was a genuine submarine capable of moving beneath the surface. After serious "teething" troubles, during which members of the crew lost their lives, the *Hunley* rammed and sank the Federal corvette, *Housatanic,* which was blockading the harbour at Charleston on February 17, 1864. J. T. E.

of bacteriological warfare. Needing to counter the overwhelming might of the United States Navy, particularly where the blockading of its ports was concerned, the South devoted much ingenuity to devising what at the time were referred to as torpedoes but which would be called mines by later generations.[6]

There were, nevertheless, some developments that would prove beneficial when peace finally came. Improvements in telegraph services speeded overland communications. Medical skills and techniques grew better, aided by a growing number of patients suffering from wounds or illnesses acquired in the field. Methods of building railroads, although primarily intended to facilitate the speedy movement of large bodies of men, animals, and supplies from place to place, were brought to a peak of efficiency that would eventually be put to more pacific use and lead to the opening of the subcontinent's interior for settlement.

Contemplating the horrors that had been released upon the land he loved with a fiery and patriotic devotion, the President wished he was still an unknown lawyer traveling the roads of Illinois in search of clients. To find oneself head of a divided nation, with brother likely to find himself fighting brother and families suffering losses on the field of battle in a cause that all too many of them only partly understood, was a far from pleasurable or satisfying occupation for a humane and kindly man. No matter what decisions were made by the one holding such a position, they could never meet with unanimous approval.

There were, the present incumbent of the White House realized, some men who claimed allegiance to the Union and who hated him and his policies as bitterly as did the most dyed-in-the-wool slavery-advocating Southron holding him alone responsible for the War Between the States.

6. An example of one way in which "torpedoes" could be used and the types involved is given in: *The Bloody Border*. J. T. E.

1
Too Rich for *Your* Blood

Unbeknown to President Abraham Lincoln, or those officials responsible for his continued safety and well-being, a group of his worst enemies among those who supported the cause of the Union were gathered at that moment not too far from where he stood brooding over the terrible state of affairs brought about by the civil conflict.

An uneasy mixture of a dozen wealthy political opportunists and "liberals" of the most viciously radical variety were assembled in the dining room of the mansion owned by George Wigg, which was situated on the opposite side of the Potomac River some distance downstream from the White House. Ostensibly, they had come together for a dinner party honoring a brigadier general visiting Washington, D. of C., to discuss with his superiors in the War Department the conducting of the less than successful campaign over which he had command. However, to anybody who knew Wigg—whose "liberal" tendencies did not include generosity where his personal worldly goods were concerned—it would have been patently obvious he was not going to such an expense for just that reason.

There was, in fact, a much more serious—some might even say treasonable—motive for the gathering.

Using the presence of Brigadier General Moses J. Buller as an excuse, Wigg had called together the group to discuss a matter which he knew they all had in mind. Like himself, every one present had no love for the present incumbent of the White House. However, such was the current popularity of the President with the masses, it would be practically impossible to have him removed from office by any constitutional or other legal means. Therefore, their host wished to sound out their thoughts about arranging an assassination, which would pave the way for the election of somebody who was closer to their own political ideals. Although he was too shrewd to make known his personal ambitions in that direction until he was better aware of their sentiments, Wigg considered himself to be the ideal candidate for the high office. With that in mind, he had grudgingly expended a considerable amount of his own money upon wining, dining, and arranging entertainment for his guests after the serious business of the evening was concluded.

However, now the meal was over, the guests, with one exception, were showing a marked reluctance to openly admit the true purpose of their visit. Possessing the mean-spirited and untrusting mentality that characterizes their kind, the "liberals" in particular were disinclined to do anything as definite as discussing in the presence of so many witnesses the ways and means to bring about that which they desired. Nor were the blatant opportunists, including the nominal guest of honor, any more willing to make declarations of intent in the company of those whom at other times they would have regarded as mortal enemies and who, furthermore, still would not hesitate to use any ill-considered or incriminating admissions against them.

"Oh, ass-hole to all this 'mother-something' pussy-footing around it!"[1] the exception shouted in the accent of a well-edu-

1. See: Paragraph Two, Author's Note. J. T. E.

cated New Englander, rising with such vehemence she sent her chair flying. "We all *know* what we're here for and the sooner we get to it the better, I say. That skinny-gutted, mealy-mouthed Sucker State jury-fixer[2] is too goddamned softhearted and softheaded to be left in office. If he has his way, he'll make peace with those peckerwood sons of bitches we're fighting at the first opportunity instead of wiping out every last mother's son of the bastards. He's *got* to be put away and there's an end to it!"

As usual, considering that her words demonstrated—despite having come from a privileged background and receiving an education at a recently opened and exclusive college for women on the outskirts of New York City—her willingness to descend to the level of the "little people," Mary Wilkinson had continued to intersperse her tirade with frequent profanities more suitable to a stableyard in moments of stress than a formal dinner in a mansion. An aspiring, albeit untalented, actress—this being an age before the profession of "liberal" ideals was a guarantee of employment, critical acclaim, and even "stardom" —she was embittered by her repeated failures on the stage and sought to relieve her disappointment by adopting the kind of unconventional behavior she considered to be the norm among thespians in Europe.

The frustrated actress did not confine her defiance of convention to lacing her speech, regardless of whose company she might be in, with foul language. Nor was it restricted to smoking cigars in public and having her yellowish brunette hair cut in a short, masculine fashion, which did nothing to relieve the harsh lines of her otherwise beautiful features. Particularly when attending formal functions where it would be considered more of an offense to the other guests than an amiably harmless eccentricity, she invariably garbed herself in male attire. How-

2. "Sucker State jury-fixer": derogatory names for respectively Illinois and a lawyer, particularly—although this did not apply in the case of Abraham Lincoln—one who was willing to employ dishonest tactics on behalf of his clients. J. T. E.

ever, this was not done with the intention of concealing her
gender. A feminist of the most volubly overbearing and over-
reacting kind, she nevertheless selected garments that left no
doubts regarding her sex.

That night, as was generally the case, the thin blue shirt
Mary was wearing beneath an open black cutaway jacket and
white riding breeches, ending in brown boots with Hessian-
pattern legs, was snug-fitting. Clinging to and emphasizing her
full bosom, its contours further defined by a scarlet silk cravat,
the nipples stood out in a way which indicated that only one
layer of material covered them. Almost tight enough to be a
second skin, the nether garments were just as successful in displaying her slender waist, curvaceous hips, and shapely thighs.
Moreover, constant practice had taught her how to exhibit the
lines of her richly feminine body, whether standing or sitting,
so that they distracted attention from the lines of arrogant superiority mingled with disdain her face invariably bore.

"He must," agreed the tall, slim, sullenly handsome, black-
haired man whose Union blue full-dress uniform bore the
"chicken" spread-eagle insignia of a colonel and had the letters
P.D. inscribed within the embroidered gold laurel wreath on
his epaulettes. "By *constitutional* means, of course!"

"By *any* goddamned means that are needed!" the yellowish
brunette insisted, just as loudly as she had made her previous
declaration. Watching Colonel Horace Trumpeter of the Pay
Department throwing a nervous glance at the closed main
doors of the dining room, she still made no attempt to hold her
voice down to the level he had employed as she continued,
"None of us here—and we all know there are plenty more like
us who feel the same way—want that miserable-looking, rebel-
loving old son of a bitch even *alive,* much less still in office,
when the war ends. Well, I have two men who can see he isn't
for us and in a way which—!"

"Hey there, Wigg!" growled the guest of honor, before any
more could be said. His voice was also that of a New Englander, albeit one of lower social origins than the feminist and
the colonel in spite of his present military rank. Showing he

was clearly sharing the misgivings of their host and the other guests, including the three young civilians she had brought with her, over the loud and incautious speech she was making, he continued as all eyes turned his way, "How well can you trust your servants?"

Around six feet in height, with longish black hair going bald on top and a bulky body running to fat, Brigadier General Moses J. Buller was in his late forties. Despite having attained so high a rank, he was not a professional soldier. He was, as he frequently mentioned, a self-made businessman whose wealth and influence had enabled him to rise swiftly in the force of volunteers formed by his home state to help maintain the Union intact. His true nature was reflected in the reddened, blue-jawed and almost porcine features that gave a clear indication of his brutal and licentious spirit. While excellently tailored, his double-breasted dark blue uniform frock coat was filled until a strain was placed upon the two rows—of eight buttons each—running down its front. Heavy with bullion, his epaulettes were embellished with a single gold star as notification of his exalted status, and were tarnished. As was the case with the coat, there were food and wine stains spattering his off-white trousers. Heavy and blunt-toed, his black boots were more suited to walking than riding a horse. Although he had a red silk sash about his bulging middle, he was not wearing a weapon belt.

"Absolutely!" the tallish, skinny, and rat-faced host of the dinner party stiffly replied, being resentful of anything which might serve to cast doubts upon him in the present company. His somber attire was eminently suitable for the successful undertaker he could claim to be, but was less suitable for the present circumstances. The garments emitted a noticeable smell of the formaldehyde-based solutions he employed in his work and was hardly conducive to a good appetite. Ignoring the fact that—like many of his kind—he kept his employees no better paid or accommodated than the "downtrodden masses" to whom he paid the same lip service as did all his guests in the

interests of obtaining political support, he elaborated, "They are completely loyal to me!"

"Be that as it may," Trumpeter grumbled, showing no sign of being convinced by the declaration and scowling his disapproval at the young woman. "I still feel it is in our own best interests that some discretion be shown in what is said!"

"Discretion!" Mary snorted, without offering to lower her voice, the word popping from her mouth as if it was causing a bad taste. Injecting the usual amount of unnecessary profanities, she went on belligerently, "If what we've come here for is too rich for *your* blood, you can always get up and walk out!"

"By God!" the colonel snarled, shoving back his chair. However, he refrained from rising or pointing out the ostensible reason for the dinner party. "You wouldn't be saying that if you were a *man!*"

"Like hell I wouldn't!" the brunette replied just as heatedly. "And don't let my being a *woman* stop you *trying* to keep me quiet. I'll meet you with swords or pistols, standing or mounted, any time you want to call me out!"

"That's easy enough for you to *say!*" Trumpeter asserted. "Even if dueling wasn't illegal, you know I couldn't fight a woman!"

"You've never got around to fighting *anybody,* if your career so far in the army is anything to go by," Mary countered disdainfully and with some justification. "But any time you're so minded, illegal or not, just say the goddamned word and I'll prove I can stand against you any way you've a mind to call it!"

Anger darkened Trumpeter's face at the words. Despite having attained rapid promotion, mainly due to possessing sufficient influential friends who were able to secure the removal to other posts of those senior to him, since enrolling as an officer he had taken great care to ensure he was never sent anywhere near the fighting lines.[3] However, while he always appeared in

3. What happened when Horace Trumpeter, promoted to Brigadier General, was sent upon active service in a fighting zone is told in: *Kill Dusty Fog!* J. T. E.

public with a revolver in his holster and a sword on the slings of his weapon belt (prompting a thirty-year veteran sergeant major with a very sound assessment of human character to spread the rumor he even wore them in bed), he had never taken the trouble to acquire skill in the use of either.

On the other hand, in addition to the conventional education supplied by the college for women she had attended, Mary had formed a sorority among students with a similar outlook on political and social issues. They had taken clandestine yet thorough instruction in subjects less usual than those offered by the official curriculum. Not only had they learned to ride astride, as well as on the socially acceptable sidesaddle, but they had taken lessons in fencing, shooting, boxing, and wrestling. Nor, having attained a standard of proficiency in such martial arts that was not equaled by her formal studies, had she forgotten what she was taught after graduation. Regarding it as a symbol of her equality with men, she had continued to keep herself in excellent physical condition and contrived to remain in practice at the acquired skills.[4]

Looking from the arrogantly scowling young woman to the glowering colonel and back, Wigg had grown increasingly alarmed as the acrimonious exchange continued. Each had adherents present, attracted to Trumpeter for the patronage he could offer, and to Mary by virtue of the sexual benefits she was willing to bestow upon those who gave her support. Already the two factions were glaring across the table at one another with thinly veiled hostility. If there should be a clash that ended in bloodshed, it would be almost impossible to keep the affair secret. Although breaches of the law against dueling were sometimes overlooked, the undertaker knew there were those in Washington who would be only too willing to use such an incident to discredit everybody even indirectly connected with it. What was more, being aware of the nature of his guests, he did not doubt the surviving losers would do all they could to en-

4. Information regarding two later graduates of the college who belonged to the sorority can be found in: *Waco's Badge* and *Hound Dog Man*. J. T. E.

compass the downfall of the winners. While he cared nothing for whatever might happen to any of them, provided he was left in the clear, he was equally certain that he would suffer in the event of trouble with the authorities.

His misgivings notwithstanding, Wigg was uncertain how he might intervene and restore order without the risk of offending one or the other group. No matter how much he might try to delude himself that he was a man of power and commanding presence, he knew he lacked the kind of forceful personality required to cope with such a potentially dangerous situation. Nor was he in such a position of authority that he could use it as a threat of personal retribution, if only by implication, to prevent the situation from worsening.

The undertaker was saved from the necessity of trying to intervene.

"Hey, now, easy on there!" Buller boomed out with an authoritative joviality, coming to his feet. "There's no call for any of us going off half-cocked!"

Although he would not have been averse to watching how an acceptance of the challenge to physical combat turned out, the general shared his host's appreciation of the advisability of preventing it from happening. Furthermore, he was quick to see how the situation might be turned to his own advantage. Despite his belief that the assassination of President Lincoln was worthy of being given serious attention and put into effect, providing a suitably safe scheme could be thought out, he had been disinclined to make a declaration upon such a dangerous issue with so many other people being party to it. Concluding that the altercation was offering him an opportunity to avoid being compelled to take a definite stand on the matter without his reticence and lack of trust becoming obvious to the others, he was wise enough to make it apparent as he intervened that he was not favoring either party.

"Come on now, everybody, let's drink to the downfall of our enemies!" Buller suggested, picking up his glass, after a few seconds had elapsed without the woman and the colonel offering to continue their angry exchange. With the toast drunk and the hostile pair seated once more, he continued, "I've got to attend a meeting with some of the general staff later this evening and will have to be leaving for it soon. So what's this entertainment you've got arranged for us, Wigg, old man?"

"Something I'm sure *you* will find most diverting, General," replied the undertaker, struggling to conceal the irritation he was experiencing over being addressed in such an excessively familiar fashion by his uncouth guest of honor. "I've heard you take an interest in such things."

"Then how's about letting us see it now?" Buller demanded rather than requested, wondering which of his interests was to be catered to and doubting that it would be one of the less salubrious kind. "Like I said, I've got this important meeting—!"

"Very well, we'll have it *now*," Wigg interrupted, accepting that he was unlikely to bring about any further discussion of the real reason for the gathering unless he offered a diversion that would give tempers a chance to cool. Picking up the bell from the table, he rang it and told the butler who came in answer to his summons, "Fetch in that woman and her girls, Barnes!"

"Very good, sir," replied the tall, graying, distinguished-looking man, and withdrew.

2

I Could Lick the Pair of Them

Returning from carrying out his instructions, the butler was accompanied by more than just "that woman and her girls." They entered on his heels, walking in a loose arrowhead formation. Following them were half a dozen of the male servants employed, much against his wishes on account of the cost, by the wife of George Wigg, who was at present on vacation in New York City. Spread along its fourteen-foot length, the men were staggering under the weight of a bulky roll of thick carpet.

Recognizing the woman in the lead, surprised exclamations burst from some of the male guests, who found it difficult to believe that their sour-faced and parsimonious host would even *know* such a person, much less invite her into his mansion while giving a dinner party, even when his wife was absent. Mary Wilkinson, although exhibiting better control over her emotions, also showed puzzlement rather than the kind of objections which might have been expected from a respectable (at

least by family background and upbringing) female member of
good society at finding herself in such unsavory company.

However, it was obvious that Brigadier General Moses J.
Buller for one guessed what was forthcoming and was looking
forward to it with considerable eagerness. He was devoting his
attention alternatively between the second and third woman
after giving a brief nod of greeting to the foremost of them.
Although he had never mentioned his taste for such a form of
entertainment to the undertaker, and wondered how it had
been discovered, he was pleased to think it was to be provided.

Peering with what appeared to be shortsighted benevolence
through gold-rimmed spectacles, as she walked demurely behind the butler, Mrs. Amy Cutler was dressed soberly and re-
spectfully in a tastefully expensive fashion. Small, white-haired
and "pleasingly plump," she had pleasant features that seemed
intended for kindly merriment. Certainly there was nothing in
her demeanor to suggest the reason for her presence. She might
have been a devoted grandmother paying a visit, or a kindly
aunt who would not hesitate before offering to care for the
children while their parents were on vacation.

Nobody who was unaware of her true status would believe
that Mrs. Cutler could put tongue to a range of profanity that
would turn an army sergeant green with envy. Or that the
benevolent-looking elderly woman was the madam of the most
exclusive and highly priced brothel in Washington. Yet both
were true. Furthermore, in addition to having established a
well-justified reputation for the cleanliness, health, honesty, discretion, and excellent behavior of her "young ladies," she
would supply certain special services to cater to the less usual
whims of those clients with sufficient money to meet her far
from niggardly charges.

Turning their respective gaze to the two much younger
women following the madam, all the guests except Buller wondered what kind of specific service they had been brought to
supply. The men considered it unlikely to be for sexual participation on their part and Mary shared their point of view. Even
with his desire to win their support, neither she nor the men

could envisage Wigg allowing such conduct on his premises. Feelings of delicacy and propriety would not have prevented him from doing so, if he believed such would serve his ends, but he would be afraid word of it might get out and have an adverse effect upon what a later generation would call his "public image."

Nothing in the appearance of the two younger women offered a clue as to why they were being brought into the dining room. Both were wrapped from neck to foot in black cloaks. While they were attractive looking, the garments prevented the formation of anything more than a general impression of the young women's figures. Looking to be in her early twenties, the girl at the right was a blonde. Her loose-hanging hair was long and showed signs of generally being plaited into braids on either side of the head. About five feet five in height, she offered a suggestion of being stocky in build, and her pretty features had a distinctly Germanic cast. About the same age, unless appearances lied, the second of them was an inch or so taller and much more beautiful. Her skin pigmentation was a rich olive brown, indicative of Latin, or at least Gallic, origins. However, her shortish, straight hair was of such a fiery red she might have dyed it that hue with a henna solution. Clearly more slender than the blonde, even though almost completely concealed by the cloak, she was lithe and possessed the grace of a dancer.

Of the guests, only Buller suspected what was going to happen. The moving of certain furniture and the unrolling of the mat, which was square in shape and a good three inches deep, gave strength to the supposition he had formed. After it was set in the corner they had cleared, so that the walls ran along two sides, the servants positioned chairs a short distance from it. With this done, they were ordered from the dining room by the butler, who, following, closed the door behind them.

"Gentlem—!" Mrs. Cutler began, after the guests had transferred from the table to the chairs at their host's request. Then, peering in her apparently shortsighted fashion—which was only a pose, her eyesight being exceptionally keen—at Mary, she gave a sniff and made an amendment with obvious disapproval. *"Lady* and gentlemen, may I present two of my young ladies who have a quarrel they wish to settle?"

"By god!" Buller breathed, piggy eyes glinting as he resumed the study of each of the "young ladies" with interest. He had heard that such "settling of quarrels" was one of the special services offered by the madam. Having a penchant for watching spectacles of that kind,[1] he added at the conclusion of his inspection, "I was *right!*"

"This is Lotte, of Germantown, Philadelphia," Mrs. Cutler claimed, ignoring the scowl of hatred being directed at her by Mary and, then her left hand indicated the redhead in the same fashion, "And Françoise, from Sault Sainte Marie, Ontario, Canada."

In response to the introductions, having walked until facing one another diagonally on the sides of the mat, the girls slowly spread open and dropped the cloaks to the floor behind them. Appreciative murmurs arose from the male guests at what was revealed by their action. All each "young lady" now wore was a sleeveless white cotton bodice with extreme décolletage, black tights, and black ballet slippers from which the hard padding of the toes had been removed. Nor did the precautions to minimize the inflicting of excessive or permanent damage while "settling their quarrel" end there. Neither wore any jewelry and their fingernails were cut short.

Each of the girls was attractive in a different kind of way. Whereas Lotte filled her skimpy costume almost to overflowing with her buxom yet curvaceously firm body, Françoise lacked her bulk. However, while much slimmer, the redhead could not be classed as skinny and flat-chested. Her bosom might fall short of the imposing bulk of the blonde's, but it was well developed for one of her build. What was more, although her

---

1. Information regarding others with a similar bizarre taste in entertainment is given in: *Old Moccasins on the Trail; Calamity, Mark and Belle;* Part Five, "The Butcher's Fiery End," J. T.'s *Ladies; Terror Valley;* Rapido Clint; *"Cap" Fog, Texas Ranger, Meet Mr. J. G. Reeder, The Sheriff of Rockabye County* and *Bad Hombre.* J. T. E.

bare arms and black-encased legs were far less obviously mus-
cled, they did not look in any way fragile. Rather the opposite,
in fact. They conveyed the impression of possessing a wiry
strength which would lend itself to considerable graceful agil-
ity.

"May the young ladies start, Mr. Wigg?" the madam inquired, having allowed a few seconds to elapse while the male
members of the audience feasted their eyes upon their companions.

"W-what?" the undertaker almost yelped, the word popping
out as if he was startled at having been addressed. Running the
tip of his tongue across his thin lips and keeping his gaze on the
far from concealed feminine attributes of the buxom blonde, he
went on hurriedly, "Yes, get them started!"

"Lotte, Françoise!" Mrs. Cutler commanded, although she
sounded more as if she were suggesting the children should go
and play in the garden rather than ordering the commencement
of a fight. "You may settle your quarrel!"

Converging in the center of the mat, which had clearly been
manufactured for such a purpose, Lotte and Françoise began to
circle, exhibiting more caution than aggression. Making ineffectual grabs with their hands, each time one made contact, she
would release the hold and jerk away as soon as it seemed the
other would lay hands upon her in return. Furthermore, on
coming to grips in response to a signal redolent of annoyance
from their employer—who had been watching the reactions of
the audience—their behavior became closer to that of a couple
of tomboy schoolgirls tussling to amuse their friends than
grown women belonging to a profession which did not call for
the possession of meek and mild spirits when seeking to settle a
quarrel by means of physical combat.

After turning around a few times on their feet and mauling
ineffectually at each other, the girls tripped. However, they
contrived to fall to the mat with far greater care than would
have been the case had they been fighting seriously and with a
mutual determination to emerge victorious. Nor was there any
more noticeable anger or efforts at inflicting pain as they began

to roll over and over, being careful to reverse direction when it seemed they would pass beyond the well-padded surface. Although they grabbed one another by the hair, neither pulled hard enough to cause suffering. They clutched at other parts of the body, too, but with just as little vigor.

"Are those tail-peddlers supposed to be *fighting*?" Mary asked, inserting a profanity before employing a derogatory term for a prostitute, having taken a seat next to Buller.

"That's what they're *sup*—!" the general commenced, finding the physical appearance of the girls more enjoyable than their efforts. Then, remembering something he had heard about the beautiful yellowish-brunette, he revised his surly comment. "Sure they're fighting. Do you reckon *you* could do any better?"

"I certainly *do*!" Mary asserted. "In fact, if that's the best they're capable of, I could lick the pair of them with one hand tied behind my back!"

"You reckon you *could,* huh?" Buller queried, his manner redolent of disbelief. "Well, *perhaps* so. Those boots would give you a hell of an edge if you *tried*!"

"Who needs the boots?" the brunette snapped, glancing with disdain at the struggling pair on the mat. "I could do it just as easily barefoot!"

"*Talk's* cheap!" the general sniffed, feigning disdain despite being delighted by the responses he was eliciting. "It's *doing* that counts!"

"If I go and do it," Mary said, eyeing Buller in a calculating fashion, "will you take me to your meeting with—the general staff?"

"Huh?" the general grunted, then stared at the brunette. "Hell, *no*!"

"Why not?" Mary challenged.

"What I'm doing is noth—!" Buller began. "I can't take a woman to meet the general staff!"

"If you don't take *me,*" the brunette replied, "I'm going to tell the general staff you've been to meet them. I'm sure they'll be most interested to hear about it!"

"How's that?" Buller snarled, his attention snapping from the still far from aggressively tussling girls.

"It's very simple," Mary claimed calmly, showing no sign of being intimidated or even slightly perturbed by the raw fury with which she was being surveyed. "I have every intention of going with you to the meeting with your 'general staff.' I want to see what—*General* Aaranovitch, shall we call him—has discovered in his laboratory that's so important it's brought you running here from Arkansas at a time when most people would think you wouldn't want to leave."

"Who the hell told you about Aarano—?" Buller began, his voice starting to rise beyond the *sotto voce* level at which he and the brunette were speaking, but he realized just in time what he was doing and brought the furiously commenced question to an uncompleted end.

"I'll tell you *after* you've let me see what 'the general staff' is up to," Mary promised, then glanced at the two girls who were still rolling about on the padded mat in their pretense at fighting. "But I'm a good sport, and to prove it, I'll still make you the same bet."

"You mean you'll go and fight the pair of them?"

"Just that!"

"Without your boots?" Buller asked, concluding he would be ill advised to refuse her demand to accompany him and, although he doubted whether he would win if all he had heard about the brunette was true, considering that accepting the wager might at least produce some more genuine action than was happening so far.

"Without them!" Mary confirmed, showing not the slightest hesitation and holding forward her right hand. "Is it a bet?"

"Yes!" Buller assented, giving the offered hand a confirmatory shake. "We've got us a bet!"

"That's what I wanted!" the brunette declared, glancing around and satisfying herself that none of the other spectators had seen or heard what was taking place. "I'll take them off and be ready in a few seconds!"

Returning to the table and sitting down, Mary watched the

girls while starting to do as she had promised. Nothing she saw
led her to change her opinion of their behavior, nor to revise
her assumption that she would not have the slightest difficulty
in winning the bet. Even if she aroused them to far greater
anger than they were displaying as they continued to turn one
another over and over across the mat, she was confident of
having sufficient ability to render both *hors de combat* without
sustaining more than minor suffering herself. On the other
hand, she reminded herself, she must not finish them off too
quickly if she was to achieve her purpose.

Ever since she had received hints that "General Aaranovitch," whom she knew to be a brilliant young chemist, was
engaged upon some kind of research for which funds had been
provided by Buller, the brunette had tried without success to
become privy to the secret. On hearing of the dinner party to be
given in honor of the general, and being aware that it had an
ulterior motive, she had decided that it offered her a chance to
make his acquaintance and she had obtained an invitation by
hinting to Wigg that her father might be induced to donate
financial backing. Her quick temper had threatened to ruin her
ambitions, but the unusual form of entertainment being provided by their host had suggested a way she might further
them. Guessing the entertainment had been selected because he
was keen on such events, she felt her participation would cause
the general to take an active interest in her. He might even
forgive her curiosity regarding his private affairs and allow her
to join his entourage. For all the less than satisfactory state of
the campaign he was conducting against the "Johnny Rebs" in
Arkansas, this would grant her a higher status than she had
been able to obtain in Washington. What was more, annoyed by
the way Mrs. Cutler had reacted on discovering she was present, she wanted to cause the madam to suffer humiliation and,
perhaps, lose at least a proportion of her fee for bringing the
"young ladies" to supposedly settle a quarrel.

After she had removed her boots, as she was never averse to
flouting what she knew to be a gorgeous and eye-catching figure
to members of the opposite sex, Mary decided to grant her male

associates some added sensual pleasure. With that in mind, she removed her coat and, taking off the cravat, unbuttoned the man's shirt to a less than decorous level. Standing up, conscious that her otherwise uncovered bosom was displayed by her actions, she stalked forward to set about what she assumed would be the easy task of winning the wager with Buller.

Startled exclamations burst from Wigg and all but one of his male guests at the sight presented by the brunette as she walked from behind them toward the mat. However, if Mrs. Cutler was alarmed or distressed by the possibility of interference with the activities of her "young ladies," she gave no sign of it. She did not so much as glance at the undertaker to discover whether he approved of what was clearly intended by Mary. Instead, she stood peering in her apparently myopic and benevolently understanding fashion to where the brunette was continuing to advance without looking back.

Although he had known what Mary was intending to do, Buller had not expected that she would discard more than the riding boots and, possibly, her jacket. Therefore, he was surprised, yet far from disapproving, of the sight she presented in passing. In fact, the removal of the cravat and the unbuttoning of the shirt was creating the kind of impression she was wanting to induce and had anticipated might be the case. Running his lascivious gaze over her as she passed, especially at the tightly filled riding breeches and the sensually hip-rolling motion she imparted to them while walking, he lost some of his resentment towards her over the intrusion into his *very* private and, he had hitherto assumed, secret affairs. Forgetting for the moment even his determination to discover and punish whoever had betrayed his confidential business, he waited with eager anticipation and hoped the two "young ladies" would survive the attentions of the brunette for long enough to supply the kind of spectacle he desired.

Much the same thought was passing through Mary's head. Although she had never engaged upon anything of the kind, her previous experiences in unarmed combat having been restricted to controlled contests against others of her kind which were never allowed to go beyond clearly defined limits, she did not doubt her ability to cope. A latent bully and sadist, she had not the slightest remorse over what she was intending to do to the blonde and the redhead. In fact, her only regret was that she would not be up against opponents anywhere near worthy of her skill.

3

This Is How She Wants It

Studying the situation as she was crossing the mat, Mary Wilkinson considered what to do about it. While she was undressing, the two "young ladies" had stopped rolling about. Still showing no greater evidence of trying to inflict pain or injuries upon one another, they were now struggling amateurishly to their feet. They appeared to be completely oblivious of her presence, probably because the possibility of intervention on the part of a guest had never entered their minds. She was confident her arrival would come as such a complete surprise she would be able to gain an advantage from which, even should they start to show a more aggressive spirit than so far, neither would have a chance to recover before she had beaten them both.

Passing around the girls, the yellowish-brunette watched the reactions of the audience as she caught each by the scruff of the neck. She saw consternation come to the face of the madam, but her main attention was devoted to Brigadier General Moses

J. Buller. Clearly he, too, was aware of what she was in a position to do and, as it would bring the affair to an immediate end, did not care for it. Therefore, despite being granted an opportunity to bang the heads of her captives together, she refrained. To have done so would undoubtedly win the bet for her. However, in addition to her desire to impress the guest of honor, her strong streak of exhibitionism and sadism refused to take the easy way out. Instead, she was determined to make the fight last as long as possible.

Using all her far from inconsiderable strength, Mary jerked the girls apart. Applying a twist and shove, she sent Françoise into the corner of the room. Using less force, she caused Lotte to take a couple of steps backward. Giving the buxom blonde no time to recover, believing she might prove the tougher of the pair, the brunette swung around to add power to a blow to her jaw. Sent twirling away, Lotte left the mat to sprawl on hands and knees at the feet of the spectators.

Having disposed temporarily of what she had estimated to be the greater threat, Mary gave her attention to the other "young lady." Showing fright, Françoise was cowering and seemed to be trying to force herself more deeply into the corner. Concluding the most she could expect would be a feeble attempt at defense or, more likely, nothing beyond a tearful pleading for mercy, the brunette strolled toward the redhead with the intention of stripping her naked if no resistance was offered. That would, at least, offer some titillation for the onlookers. The humiliation might also goad the slender girl into essaying some form of offensive action to keep the men entertained until the blonde was able to return to the fray.

Suddenly, while Mary was drawing her conclusions, Françoise's demeanor underwent a startling transformation. The expression of fear departed from the beautiful face, being replaced by one of determination mingled with a suggestion of mockery. Before the brunette could fully comprehend what might be implied by the change, the redhead thrust herself from the confines of the corner. Rising with an almost balletic grace, her left leg passed between the reaching hands of her intended attacker. Caught beneath the right breast with some force, by the ball of the foot instead of the toes, a squeal of pain burst from Mary. Her overconfident advance was turned into a retreat, but she was not permitted to retire unimpeded.

Showing none of the hesitancy that had characterized the opening stages of her "fighting" with Lotte, Françoise displayed much greater skill than had formerly been the case. The moment her foot returned to the ground, she pivoted upon it. As she was doing so, moving with an equal speed and grace, her right leg flashed out horizontally. Kicked in the stomach, by a limb powered with muscles like those of a ballet dancer in full training, Mary gasped and folded at the middle. She felt a hand sink into her short hair and another grasp the waistband of her riding breeches. Subjected to a surging heave, which warned that the muscular development of the lissome redhead was not solely confined to the legs, she was sent twirling into the corner from which her assailant had erupted. However, as she had straightened instinctively, only her left shoulder took the impact.

The unexpected kicks and collision had caused suffering, but Mary was far from rendered *hors de combat.* To give her credit, obnoxious though she was in many ways, she had considerable courage and fortitude. Added to a naturally competitive spirit, these qualities revolted against the thought of letting herself be seen to go down in defeat. What was more, a further inducement arose from the realization that she could have been deliberately tricked into her far from enjoyable situation. Remembering how she had frequently boasted of her fighting prowess and bewailed the lack of worthwhile opponents, Wigg—or perhaps Colonel Horace Trumpeter—might have arranged for Mrs. Amy Cutler to supply the two "young ladies" ostensibly to "settle a quarrel" between them, the real reason being to have her become embroiled. That would explain the poor display they had been giving. Therefore, if the assumption was correct, whoever was responsible would now be hoping to see her receive a humiliating thrashing.

Aroused to an even greater pitch of fury by her suppositions,

Mary flung herself to meet the approaching redhead. She was
behaving with a recklessness that could have caused her greater
grief than proved to be the case. Swerving at the last moment,
Françoise once again avoided being clutched by the talonlike
hands of the brunette. However, on this occasion, there was no
retaliatory kick. Instead, grabbing Mary by the hair and back
of the shirt as her impetus compelled her to blunder by, Françoise brought her to a halt. Offered no chance to struggle
against the holds, much less escape, she was swung around.
Feeling the buttons that she had left fastened burst off and the
shirt being dragged out of the riding breeches, she was spun
and returned to the corner. Only by thrusting her arms before
them was she able to prevent her face and bosom from striking
the wall.

Despite having contrived to reduce the danger of her arrival,
Mary knew she was still far from out of trouble. Keeping her
arms raised protectively, as she had been taught during boxing
instruction at college, she turned to defend herself against
whatever her surprisingly efficient opponent might be contemplating. Peering warily between them, she saw the slender girl
approaching with all the latent menace of a cat preparing to
torment a crippled mouse. The savage determination still
played upon the beautiful olive brown features, warning she
was in deadly earnest and meant to show as little mercy as it
had been intended would be given to her.

What was more, to Mary's fast-growing perturbation, the
advance was not being made in the kind of wild rush with
hands reaching for hair that she had anticipated and was confident she could counter, through superior skill, to regain the
initiative. Instead, Françoise's fists were clenched, the right
held just below eye level and the left in line with the *solar
plexus*. This, the brunette knew, allowed the right arm to act as
guard against higher and the left to offer protection from lower
blows. Added to the way her dancing steps were taken up on
the toes, everything indicated that the redhead was a much
more experienced fighter than was envisaged. Furthermore, her
competence was in a masculine rather than a feminine fashion.

Her posture and tactics were derived from the French style of boxing known as *savate*, in which kicking supplemented punching with the fists.

Such a discovery was far from pleasant for Mary, prior comments about the dearth of worthwhile opponents notwithstanding. Nor, regardless of her desire to entertain and earn the approbation of Buller, was she enamored of the prospect that she was up against at least one far more competent antagonist than she had imagined when making the wager. However, if not exactly salvation, a respite was granted before she was called upon to take any action against Françoise.

Having lifted Lotte to her feet on receipt of an order from the general, Lieutenants Martin Flannery and Robert Cryer—who had been brought to the dinner party in their capacity as his *aides-de-camp*—felt her start to struggle. Before she could do anything more to free herself, they propelled her onto the mat with a surging heave. Although she had intended to turn upon them and demonstrate her resentment of the intrusion, she changed her mind on seeing where she was going. Giving a hiss of satisfaction, she continued to move toward the corner.

"Shall I stop them?" Mrs. Cutler asked, looking at Wigg.

"What for?" Buller inquired, before his host could speak. Being certain the brunette would insist upon learning more about his secret affairs even if she lost, he felt she should at least be compelled to earn the knowledge. "This is how she wants it. She reckoned she could lick the pair of them, so let us give her the chance."

"Very well," Wigg acceded, concluding the general also wanted to see how the intrusion by Mary would turn out and having no fond feelings for her since her temper had ruined his plans for the evening. "Let's see how she gets on against them."

"As you wish," the madam accepted. "Just so long as my young ladies and I aren't held responsible for whatever happens to her."

"You won't be," Buller promised and Wigg muttered his agreement.

Having arrived within reaching distance while the conversa-

tion was taking place, Lotte clearly considered the interference
by the brunette took precedence over whatever difference of
opinion she might have had with Françoise. Despite the claim
that she had a quarrel to settle, she did nothing more offensive
than grab and push the other "young lady" aside. Having sent
the redhead reeling across the mat, she sank her fingers into the
short hair of the visitor and tugged with a vigor she had not
displayed earlier. Unfortunately for her, the locks she was
grasping lacked sufficient length to produce the most painful
results. The pulling hurt, but only enough to provoke the recipient into making a more positive kind of response. Bringing her
arms from the protective posture, which had proved valueless
against the method of attack her present assailant was employing, Mary sent a punch with each clenched fist into the body of
the shorter "young lady." Despite the rubbery hardness of her
midsection, which testified to her excellent physical condition,
Lotte gasped and her fingers lost their hold.

Throwing up her left fist as she was released, Mary sent it in
an uppercut to the imposing bosom of the blonde. Although it
elicited a croaking cry of pain, the blow failed in its primary
purpose. Rocking on her heels instead of retreating, Lotte retal-
iated with a roundhouse slap, which left a red handprint on the
cheek of the guest. Squealing in anger, Mary forgot her training
and responded in the same fashion. Unlike herself, Lotte was
able to move away on being struck. However, before the brunette could capitalize upon her advantage, there was an interruption.

Running from where she had been pushed, Françoise showed
a similar disinclination to "settle a quarrel" with the other
"young lady." Instead, bounding into the air with legs spread
apart, she placed her hands upon the stocky shoulders and
went over the blonde as if playing leapfrog. Alighting in front
of Mary, she caught a second slap which was intended for
Lotte. As her head was jolted around, she was placed in jeopardy. Grabbing the shoulder straps of Françoise's white cotton
bodice, the brunette jerked them around until they pinioned the
redhead's arms below the elbows. Not only did the tight-fitting

material grip and render defense with the hands impossible, but
Françoise's firm breasts were bared by the pull downward.
However, as had been the case with Lotte, Mary was not allowed to make the most of the opportunity she had created.
Taking her hand from the cheek slapped by the intruder, the
blonde once again caught and heaved the redhead out of the
way. Having done so, she lunged to grab the brunette by the
hair. Pure reflex caused Mary to behave in a like manner as she
felt as if the top of her head was being ripped off. While starting
to pull, she also contrived to shove herself from the corner.
Spinning around, tugging and jerking at the hair they were
grasping, she and the blonde blundered toward the third
woman.

Being unable to use her hands to retain her balance, Françoise tripped. The thick padding of the mat saved her from
injury, or even being temporarily incapacitated by the landing.
Seeing the other two approaching, she made no attempt to return the bodice to its previous position. Instead, wriggling her
arms upward, she liberated them, leaving herself bare to the
waist. Nor was she a moment too soon. Swinging one another
around without watching where they were going, Lotte and
Mary were on the point of trampling her underfoot. Rolling
clear of the embattled pair, she came to her knees. Diving to
catch them both around the legs, she brought them down in a
sprawling heap. However, before she could get clear, each
made an involuntary grab for her. Caught by the hair and the
displaced bodice, she was dragged into a squirming mass of
struggling femininity that displayed none of the scientific fighting employed earlier.

The spectacle created by the latest development was one that
the watching men found amusing and not without erotic attrac-
tion. Three divergent types of female pulchritude were shown,
each at its respective best by comparison with the other two.
This was enhanced when, seeking to inflict suffering by any
means available, wildly clutching hands tore off Lotte's bodice
and ripped away the already damaged shirt to leave Mary clad
in breeches, which suddenly split along the back seam to show

scarlet silk underpants and black stockings. Nor was it a matter
of being two against one. Despite their earlier reluctance to
fight, Lotte and Françoise were now treating each other just as
roughly as they did the beautiful brunette. Furthermore, despite the disparity in their weights, they appeared evenly
matched. The redhead was fast, surprisingly strong, and with
gymnastic ability which came close to that of a contortionist in
making use of her slender, wiry body. On the other hand, for all
her bulk, the buxom blonde proved remarkably agile. Nor, although it was her first involvement in such a fracas, were the
efforts of the brunette to be despised.

After having crossed the mat twice in their mindless mauling, pure chance each time causing them to reverse direction
when the edge was reached, the trio struggled onto their knees
at one of the open sides. Caught by a swinging punch from
Lotte, Mary was toppled to the floor. Being granted a chance to
do so, Françoise sprang to her feet and retreated to the center
of the mat. Spitting obscenities in English and German, the
blonde started to rise almost as quickly. Glaring around as she
rubbed the back of her hand across her face and saw the blood
it had collected from her nostrils, she was clearly meaning to
charge at the redhead.

Although, as when tussling with Lotte at the beginning,
Françoise had not been showing any of the skill used against
Mary, once they were all fighting on the mat, she proved it was
no fluke that had allowed her to cope so well. Going to meet
the blonde, she crouched beneath the reaching hands. Hooking
her arms around Lotte's knees and snapping them together, she
exhibited the wiry strength her slender body was capable of
producing by lifting her captive. Swung around and thrown
backward, the blonde staggered on landing. Going over the
edge of the mat, she sat down on the floor. Winded by her
descent, she was helpless to protect herself. Darting across, the
redhead kicked her under the chin. Pitching onto her back, she
sprawled supine and unmoving.

Forcing herself onto hands and knees, Mary was wishing she
had never allowed herself to be tricked—as she was now con-

vinced she had been—into fighting. What she had gone through during the thrashing, churning brawl on the mat went far beyond anything in her previous experience. No boxing or wrestling bout in which she had engaged at college had ever been conducted with such primeval savagery. However, she was given no option over whether to continue. As they had when Lotte was first sent to the floor, Flannery and Cryer obeyed a signal from their superior. Going forward, they raised the gasping brunette to her feet. Giving her just as little chance of resisting, or expressing her views on the matter, they thrust her toward where the redhead was rendering the buxom blonde *hors de combat*.

Retreating to the center of the mat, Françoise reverted to the tactics employed when first meeting an attack by Mary. While the exertions she had undergone had slowed her to some extent, the same applied even more so to the brunette. Stepping aside as Mary tried to grab her, she snapped a kick to the stomach and pivoted to send another to the split open seat of the ruined white breeches. Driven against the wall, the brunette turned and shoved herself away with hands reaching more to fend off the approaching redhead than for taking offensive action. Ducking beneath them, Françoise butted her in the chest and she went back once more into the corner. Rebounding helplessly, she collided with the still lowered head. Feeling her legs encircled by the wiry arms, she was lifted and forced to turn a half somersault over her assailant, then landed flat on her back.

Partially dazed by the fall, although the padding of the mat had served its function by reducing the impact, Mary was still sufficiently in possession of her faculties to counter what was intended to happen next. Stepping around, Françoise raised her right foot. Before she could stamp with it, acting upon a primitive instinct for self-preservation rather than through conscious memories of lessons in unarmed combat, the brunette grabbed for and caught her by the ankle. Thrusting herself into a sitting position, Mary gave a twisting heave at the captured limb. Shoved away, the redhead was unable to avoid falling to her hands and knees. While this was happening, taking Lotte by

the ankles and drawing her away from the mat, Mrs. Cutler
covered her with one of the cloaks, then resumed watching the
fight.

By the time the redhead was up, so was the brunette. Although Mary was now thoroughly frightened and wanted to get
away, she was not allowed to. Françoise clearly intended to
stop her from leaving. She lunged in the desperate hope of
battering a passage by sheer weight. The attempt failed miser-
ably and painfully. Meeting her instead of dodging, the fists of
the redhead felt like knobs of bone without any covering of
flesh as they drove into her bosom, stomach, or face. Oblivious
of the increasingly wild punches being landed in return, Françoise kept up her unremitting punishment of the heavier girl.

Going into what would have been a clinch in boxing, the
brunette sought to restrain the redhead from continuing the
rain of blows. In her struggle to escape, Françoise somehow
managed to interlock fingers with Mary, and they commenced
a primitive trial of strength. Earlier in the fight, this would have
proved advantageous to the more weighty brunette. Now she
was feeling the effects of the strenuous brawl. The same applied
to the slender redhead, but she had suffered less and was in
even better physical condition than her opponent. For all that,
she did not have things all her own way. Gasping for breath,
blood from their nostrils splashing unheeded off their chins
onto heaving bare bosoms and being washed away by the copi-
ous perspiration each was shedding, they devoted all their en-
ergy to the struggle. First one would be compelled to move
back a few steps, then she would contrive to bring herself to a
halt and the other would have to retire a short way.

At last, almost as if receiving and acting upon a signal, the
young women snatched their hands free. Stumbling apart, each
essayed a punch with such vigor that—on missing the intended
targets—they turned in a mutually involuntary circle. For once,
Mary came off best. Linking her fingers as she went, she
slammed the interlocked fists between the slender bare shoulders to send Françoise in a reeling sprawl that ended in a kneeling posture facing the corner of the room. About to flee, the

brunette saw what she believed to be a chance to prevent the redhead from following. Moving forward exhaustedly on spraddled-apart feet, ready to turn and run if the other showed any sign of rising, Mary grabbed her from behind by the hair and one shoulder with the intention of crashing her head against the wall.

Watching what was happening, the spectators brought their vociferous encouragement of the respective combatants to an end. It seemed that, in spite of all she had suffered at the hands of the redhead, the brunette was going to be victorious. Their feelings were mixed as they reached the conclusion. No matter whether for or against such a result, all knew Mary would be even more insufferable after winning.

Feeling herself gripped, Françoise was galvanized into motion. Realizing she could not escape from the fingers buried into her hair, she gave a sudden twisting writhe, and the other hand was unable to retain its grip upon her sweat-soddened shoulder. Bringing her right arm from supporting her against the wall, she bent and drove it backward. As she was struck between her spread-apart thighs, a strangled moan burst from the brunette and she staggered away from her apparently helpless intended victim. Collapsing to her knees in the center of the mat, she clutched at the stricken area and doubled over keening in torment.

Rising, the redhead went after Mary. Grasping her by the hair with both hands and dragging her erect, Françoise held her head up in the left and swung a roundhouse right cross to her jaw. Spun around and sent tottering away, she rammed bosom-first into the wall. Flattened against it, she was starting to slide down when she was pulled around. Completely helpless and defenseless, she could barely raise a moan as a knee was driven into her stomach. Crumpling forward, she wrapped her arms mindlessly around those of the slender redhead. Throwing them off without difficulty, despite clearly being close to exhaustion, Françoise stepped away and allowed the brunette to topple face forward to the mat. Moving until standing astride her, the redhead rolled her over and, gripping her sweat-matted hair, drew her into a sitting position. About to hit her again, Françoise realized it was not necessary. On being released, Mary flopped back flaccidly and unconscious.

4

You Can't Take *Her* With *Us*

"What a fight *that* was, by God!" Brigadier General Moses J. Buller enthused, leading some of the spectators onto the mat. His porcine features were glistening with perspiration and his gaze ran lasciviously over the half-naked victress. "You whipped her real good, Frenchie!"

"I always try to 'whip her real good,' as you say, *M'sieur le General*," Françoise answered breathlessly. Her English was heavily accented in the French fashion, as might be expected of one who had been introduced by such a name and who came from Sault Sainte Marie, Ontario, Canada. Swaying with exhaustion, but making no attempt to conceal her bare bosom from the blatantly lecherous scrutiny of the guest of honor or attempting to stanch the blood that dribbled from her nostrils, she darted a glance at Mrs. Amy Cutler and went on, "There is *nothing* I enjoy so much as fighting with another woman, particularly when I am not given the order to hold back."

"There isn't, huh?" Buller said pensively, finding the information interesting and concluding the madam had instructed her two "young ladies" merely to make a pretense at fighting.

"Nothing, *M'sieur le* General," the slender redhead confirmed and waved a hand toward the motionless, apart from the heaving unclad bosom, figure at her feet. "But I hope I did not do the wrong thing in beating this lady?"

"She brought it all on herself!" Buller asserted. Having swung a coldly challenging glare toward the three young men who had accompanied Mary Wilkinson and receiving no response, he continued, "Didn't she, Wigg?"

"W—!" the undertaker began, but realized he was likely to antagonize either the brunette or the general no matter which way he replied. Deciding that the latter wielded a much greater authority and was clearly in favor of what had happened, he finished, "Miss Wilkinson must have known the risks involved when she took it upon herself to join the fighting. I hardly think we can blame this young woman for defending herself when she was attacked."

"That's how *I* see it too!" Buller declared, once again glaring at the brunette's adherents, and his tone warned he would brook no objections. Then he looked at Mrs. Cutler and continued in a milder manner, "Just as soon's she's ready to go, I'm taking Frenchie here out to dinner with me, Amy."

"I must admit Françoise has certainly earned such a treat, General," the madam replied, nodding her head in approval. Draping the other cloak over the exhaustion-slumped shoulders of the slender redhead and moving her away from the supine brunette, she went on, "So, providing she feels up to accepting your most kind invitation, of course, I don't have the slightest objection to her going to dinner with you."

"I feel up to it, *Tante* Amy!" the beautiful girl claimed eagerly, if still more than a trifle breathlessly. Without making any attempt to draw the long black garment around her and conceal her perspiration-soaked, bruised, sore-looking and otherwise unclad torso, she smiled at Buller in a conspiratorial fashion and announced, "I would like nothing *more* than to go to—*dinner*—with you, *M'sieur le* General."

"Then that is settled, my dear," Mrs. Cutler claimed, and waving a hand to where the buxom blonde from Germantown, Philadelphia, was groaning and stirring beneath the cloak that was covering her, she went on briskly, "If you would be so good as to have somebody carry poor Lotte for me, Mr. Wigg, I will go and help Françoise make ready to leave with the general."

"You do just that, Amy!" the burly guest of honor authorized, giving his host no chance to express a point of view at the request. Taking a bulging wallet from the inside pocket of his double-breasted full-dress blue Union Army tunic, he extracted some banknotes and, handing them to the madam, instructed, "Have her ready to go as fast as you can. I don't want to be late getting to—!"

"You can't take *her* with *us*!" protested First Lieutenant Martin Flannery.

In spite of his name, the speaker's saturnine features had lines more suggestive of Mid-European than Celtic origins. Tall, slim, with long black hair, his accent was Connecticut rather than Irish and implied he came from the same area as the general. However, in addition to the possession of considerable wealth, he was also of a higher social status than the general.

"David Aarano—!" commenced the shorter, close to portly, pallid, and surly-featured Second Lieutenant Robert Cryer, running a pudgy hand nervously through long brown hair going thin on top, his voice suggesting he was of a similar background and birthplace to Flannery.

The uniforms worn by the protestors were cut in a fashion indicating they served with one of the regiments formed purely to take part in the War Between the States and were therefore superior to the dictates of the *Manual of Dress Regulations* for the regular army. While Union blue in color, the waist-long and tail-less "dolman" jacket had lines of gold braid across the chest and was trimmed with white fur. A "barreled" sash around the waist had cords, "barrels," and tassels of gold. Tight-fitting, the light blue riding breeches disappeared into black "Napoleon" leg boots, the tops of which extended to above knee-level at the front. Removed on their arrival at the mansion, each black fur *"colpack"* busby hat had a red "bag," with piping, tasseling and "raquette" hanging cords of gold. The heavy brass badge, based on the coat of arms of their home state, was surrounded by the lettering NEW HAMPSTEAD VOLUNTEERS and was, in each case, tarnished and unpolished.

"When I want advice from either of you, I'll ask for the son of a bitch!" Buller interrupted, his savage glare having brought the less than cautious words of the junior lieutenant to a halt. "If I say she's coming, that means she *comes.*"

"But—*sir*—!" Flannery began, cheeks reddening.

"M'sieur le General!" Françoise put in, with a mixture of politeness and petulance. "If my presence will not be acceptable to these two young officers, who I assume are under *your* command, I will abide by *their* wishes and, much as I was looking forward to it, will forget about coming to—*dinner*—with you."

"I said I was taking you, so that's what I'm going to do!" Buller replied in tones of grim finality, despite having started to experience second thoughts regarding the advisability of having issued the invitation. His assertion was prompted by the fact that he had had to glower at Flannery before he was accorded his due honorific, and also by the realization that to change his mind so soon after making his declaration would convey the impression to the other guests that he was allowing his actions to be dictated by his subordinates. "Cryer, you go and make sure the coach will be ready for us in—?"

"An hour," supplied Mrs. Cutler, although the general had glanced in an interrogative fashion at the redhead standing by her side.

"As always, *Tante* Amy is being far too kind and considerate," Françoise declared, wrapping her cloak around her. "Your meeting with the general staff is clearly a matter of urgency, *M'sieur le* General, so I can be ready to leave in not more than thirty minutes providing I can have the first use of *M'sieur* Wigg's *douche* bath."

"You can do that all right," Buller assented, again without offering to consult his host. "I've always heard the victor gets the spoils and you sure as shit was the victor. So thirty minutes it is. Make sure the coach is ready and waiting by then, *Mister* Cryer!"

"Yes—sir!" the junior of the lieutenants answered sullenly, requiring an angry scowl from the general before he added the second word.

"And what about Lotte, General?" the madam prompted, as Cryer was stalking away, followed by Flannery.

"Horace!" Buller barked. "Seeing's how my aides are busy, ha—will you have your men carry the gal for Mrs. Cutler?"

"If you wish, sir," Colonel Horace Trumpeter replied, after a brief pause to glance at his obviously willing companions, and knowing he had been given an order regardless of how it was worded. "See to it, gentlemen."

"Thank you, gentlemen," Mrs. Cutler said. "Come along, Françoise. Mr. Baxter will show us to the bathroom."

"Hey, there, you fellers!" the general called, directing the words at the three young men in civilian clothing who had gathered around and were examining the battered and still unconscious brunette. "When Miss Wilkinson comes round enough to know what you're saying, tell her even though she's lost her bet I'll let her know what happens at my meeting with the general staff if she drops by at my hotel in the morning."

"Bet?" queried the tallest of the three.

"She'll know what it's all about!" Buller snapped. "Just you make sure she gets my message!"

Neither a sense of honor nor a feeling of respect for a gallant fighter was responsible for the invitation. Although the general had not met Mary prior to the dinner party, nothing he had seen or heard about her led him to assume she would prove a good loser. Suspecting she would be in a most vindictive mood when she regained her faculties and might even think he had tricked her into becoming involved, hoping that she would be seriously injured, he was trying to prevent her from carrying out her threat of reporting him to the general staff. He could not believe she had any definite information, but realized she might fabricate something that would cause an investigation into his affairs. Should this eventuate, his secret would almost certainly be discovered. Being, with a few exceptions, men of honor, his superiors would neither approve nor sanction the methods of waging war that the young chemist he had financed claimed to have discovered, and which had brought him to Washington.

"I want that old whorehouse madam and both her pox-ridden tail-peddlers killed!" Mary Wilkinson profanely informed the two young men riding with her in the hired coach that was taking them away from the—as she now regarded it—disastrous dinner party given by George Wigg. She had gone there filled with confidence that she would be invited to participate in high, if not legal, matters of national policy, and she was leaving in the knowledge that she was now unlikely ever to be even taken seriously by her fellow conspirators after what they had seen happen to her. A savage bitterness filled her voice and the obscenities she uttered did not seem out of place. "And I want it done tonight!"

Huddled upon the forward seat of the vehicle, the formerly sensual and sulky beauty of the yellowish-brunette was marred by her left eye being puffed until no more than a discolored slit, her nose and top lip being swollen, and her now ashy-gray features looking haggard. Her whole posture indicated that she was still experiencing the effects of the beating she had taken. Nor was the sensation in any way lessened by the remembrance that the punishment had been inflicted by the slender redhead she had believed would prove a helpless victim with whom she could play like a cat tormenting a mouse.

Over an hour had elapsed between Mary having regained consciousness and being able to stand unaided. Even then, every movement she made was a source of agony. Only the bitter hatred she was feeling toward the three women she held jointly responsible for her suffering and humiliation had supplied the inducement she needed to clean herself in the *douche* bath and

dress in a shirt and pair of trousers borrowed from her host.
Light though it was, the touch of the former garment had
caused such added pain to her bruised bosom and sore torso
that she had not donned her cravat and cutaway coat before
leaving the mansion. In fact, she was so filled with self-pity she
had failed to notice that certain orders she had issued were
being ignored. Instead, boarding the carriage with two of her
companions, she had waited until they had left the grounds
before making known her wishes.

"Oh Christ, Mary!" Eric Lubbock protested in his near-
whining Mid-West accent. "W-We can't do *that*!"

"It—It's too damned risky!" claimed Martin Blick, sounding
just as alarmed by the prospect.

The pair, and Alister Graham, the third member of Mary's
coterie, were much alike in physique and mentality. All were
tallish, lean, sallow-faced, with long hair and straggly beards.
Claiming to have such poor eyesight it precluded enrollment in
the armed forces and actually going to fight the Southrons for
whom they professed a mutually vociferous hatred, each wore
spectacles when in public. They "served" the Union by acting
as correspondents for radical newspapers and made certain
they were never sent on assignments that might place their
respective lives in jeopardy. All gave their adherence to the
brunette because of her willingness to be sexually forthcoming,
rather than out of any feelings of respect for her beliefs. Each
was, however, more under her thumb than any cared to admit.

"Don't be alarmed, *darlings*!" Mary snapped, having no illu-
sions so far as the courage—or lack of it—of her companions
was concerned. "I don't expect either of you, or Alister, to do
the killing. After you've dropped me off at the hotel, fetch
Blunkett and Kendall to me."

"Blunkett and Kendall?" Blick repeated, showing no enthusiasm.

"Yes!" the brunette confirmed. "I didn't have a chance to
mention them to Wigg because of that yellow-bellied bastard
Trumpeter, so they might as well do something for me to earn
their son-of-a-bitching keep!"

"You can't do *anything* to that redhaired girl who bea—!" Lubbock began, then decided to rephrase what he had realized just in time would have been a most tactless comment under the circumstances. "To that French-Canadian girl."

"Why not?" Mary demanded, and it was obvious she was needing to exercise considerable self-control to hold back anger over what had almost been said.

"Buller took her with him," Blick explained, as the other correspondent looked at him for support. "Even if we knew where they've gone—!"

"How the hell do you mean, *'Even if we knew'*?" Mary hissed, glaring savagely at her companions. "Alister is following them, like I told him—isn't he?"

"Well, no," Blick admitted. "There wasn't any need after what Buller told us."

"Well, isn't that just too goddamned *kind* of him!" Mary sneered, showing no excess of pleasure, when she had received the message relayed from the general. "But the only way he's going to have me keep quiet is by letting me in on whatever he's up to with Aaranovitch—and letting me *kill* that scraggy redhaired whore with my bare hands!"

While Mary Wilkinson was describing the terms she intended to demand as the price of her silence, Buller and his party were approaching their destination. What he had learned during the journey increased his hopes that the visit would prove worthwhile.

On leaving the dining room at Wigg's mansion, the redhead had kept to the schedule she had set herself. What was more, she had clearly made the most of the thirty minutes that she stipulated was all she would need to prepare herself. While away, she had contrived to stop the bleeding from her nostrils, washed away the perspiration and grime in the *douche* bath, very successfully concealed the few marks on her face that had accrued during the fight, dressed, and before the time had expired, been ready to take her departure.

Although he had heard something of the exceptionally high

standards required by Mrs. Amy Cutler of her "young ladies," particularly with regard to the way they had to dress when outside the brothel, Buller had been pleasantly surprised by what he saw on the slender girl when she returned from performing her ablutions. Her garments had been as stylishly elegant, tasteful, and respectable as those of the madam. Nor had she appeared ill at ease, or out of place, wearing them.

Clad as she now was in a black two-piece traveling costume and frilly-bosomed white silk blouse—which set off without blatantly flaunting her lissome and curvaceous figure—with the sharp toes of black high-button shoes just visible beneath the hem of the skirt, Françoise might have been an invited guest rather than an employee of a brothel hired to provide an unusual form of entertainment at the dinner party. A large white straw "Lavinia" hat, secured by a blue satin band that passed under the chin and by a bow on top of the crown, prevented her shorter-than-fashionable hair from being seen. The dainty, furled light blue parasol and small, matching reticule she was carrying would have been just as acceptable in polite society as her attire and modest amount of facial makeup. Nor would the bulky gold ring on the second finger of her left hand and the broad bracelet—of obvious foreign manufacture and apparently made from silver—around her right wrist be unsuitable as jewelry for a "good" woman.

Studying the appearance of the beautiful redhead, Buller concluded she was even better suited for the purpose he had in mind than he had first envisaged. As had frequently happened prior to his entering the army, either because they shared his taste in such a bizarre form of entertainment or wished to ingratiate themselves by pandering to his whims, acquaintances in Arkansas had sought to produce women willing to fight before him. Such events had become as regular occurrences at his headquarters as they had formerly been in his home. There was considerable betting on the bouts, so he, too, was always on the lookout for contenders.

Having seen how competently Françoise had behaved in combat against two heavier opponents, the general had already decided she could be of use to him when he heard her comment saying how much she enjoyed fighting. He had seen there were added advantages when he discovered that, unlike the usual type of contender procured by himself or his associates, she could convey the impression of being a "good" woman, present as one of the guests rather than having been hired to perform. Nor had the information he had acquired from her on the journey led him to revise his opinion.

Such was the secrecy Buller felt it advisable to employ that despite having enlisted men in his entourage who were far more competent at driving, he had delegated the task of driving the coach to his junior *aide-de-camp*. With the possibility of the distant storm approaching, Flannery had been far from pleased when informed he was to ride on the box with Cryer instead of inside. However, although he had drawn the correct conclusion with regard to the seating arrangements, the reason for them had failed to come to fruition.

On placing an arm around her shoulders as a prelude to even more intimate fondling, although she had shown little sign of aftereffects from the fight, Buller had been told by the redhead that she only responded to the kind of pain caused by such treatment when she was in bed. Normally, he would have ignored the comment, but was sufficiently impressed by her potential as a fighter to refrain rather than chance antagonizing her. Her next remarks had implied the result would be well worth waiting for until his business was completed and they could return to his suite at the hotel.

If Françoise had been interested in where they were going, the blinds being pulled down at all the windows, she had given no sign of it. Instead, she had told the general enough to increase his desire to have her accompany him when he returned to Arkansas. She had said she adopted her present way of life due to the death of her parents leaving her with little money. Having no training for earning a respectable living, she had decided to put her proclivity for fighting—developed in a tomboy childhood—to use. Finding the only way to do so was via people like Mrs. Cutler, she had gained experience in Canada before coming to the United States in search of more lucrative employment. However, while such combat stimulated her sexually, she was not a prostitute. It was her ambition to find a wealthy patron for whom she could contend, offering him the benefits of the stimulation, instead of needing to work out of a brothel. Doing the latter, she had asserted, generally resulted in being given opponents who were afraid of getting hurt. This caused the kind of restrictions being placed upon her which required playing at fighting such as had happened with Lotte, and she was grateful for the intervention by the female guest as it allowed her to show how competently she could perform. Satisfied he had found what he wanted, Buller had offered to be her sponsor. Much to his annoyance, he found she had reservations over accepting. These stemmed from his reason for visiting Washington.

Although the War Between the States was progressing favorably for the Union almost everywhere else, this did not apply in Arkansas. There, opposed by a force that had access to superior sources of supply than those available to other regions of the South, and who were fighting a campaign ideally suited to the temperament of many of its members, the Johnny Rebs were doing far more than just holding their ground. To be fair to Buller, however, this state of affairs was not of his making. He was placed in command, he had come to suspect, because no other general wanted the task, due to his predecessor being abducted from what should have been a safe camp by a Confederate cavalry patrol and carried off as a prisoner.[1] Nor, despite his undoubted ability as a businessman and organizer in civilian life, had he proved any better able to even reduce the constant attrition caused by raids from similar patrols employing tactics modeled upon those of the "horse Indians" of Texas, against whom many of them had frequently been in contention prior to enlisting to fight the "Yankees."

That Françoise should have known of the difficulties facing Buller had not struck him as suspicious, or even come as any

1. Told in: *The Big Gun.* J. T. E.

great surprise. In spite of attempts made by his predecessor to prevent news of what was happening being spread, it had done so, and was common knowledge in Washington. What had annoyed him was her declaration that, interesting as she had found his proposition, she felt it would be unsafe to accompany him to Arkansas. Wanting to relieve her anxieties, he had explained that he was on his way to see a man who would help solve his predicament. When he had confessed he did not know exactly what form the relief would take, she had remained reluctant to accept his offer. When she had admitted she would otherwise have been willing to accept his patronage, despite having another potential sponsor safely ensconced in Washington, he had promised she could accompany him and see for herself the discovery made by David Aaranovitch.

"We've arrived—*sir!*" Flannery announced, with the slight delay he always made before applying the honorific. He descended from the box of the Concord coach, which had come to a halt shortly after the promise had been made, and had thrown open the left side door. Directing a scowl redolent of hostile disapproval at the second occupant, he added, without consulting his superior officer or offering to remove his *colpack* headdress as a sign of respect for her sex, "You'll have to stay in there until we're through."

"*Sacré bleu.* How strange are the ways of the United States Army, *M'sieur le* General," the redhead commented. Paying not the slightest discernible attention to the man who had addressed her, she elaborated in a polite tone which was nevertheless underlaid with resentment and annoyance, "In the army of my country, a subordinate officer would *never* take it upon himself to give *orders* to the guest of his *superior* without at least *asking* whether they met with the approval of his *superior.*" She paused for a moment, then shrugged and concluded, "But if such is the way in your country, even though you did promise to take me in to see this wonderful discovery of the chemist you *personally* have hired, I will stay here as the *lieutenant* orders."

"You're coming with me, Frenchie!" Buller declared, despite having considered asking the redhead to remain in the coach

until he had ensured Aaranovitch was justified in the claims
made for his discovery. Antagonism over the thinly veiled dis-
respect accorded to him by Flannery, combined with a desire to
make a suitable impression upon Françoise, caused him to revise his decision. Silencing with a prohibitive glare the protest
his subordinate was on the point of making, he rose and continued in tones of finality, "Come on. We'll go take a look!"

5

This Will Win the War

Brigadier General Moses J. Buller having indicated that she should leave ahead of him, Françoise paused for a moment on reaching the open door of the Concord coach. Showing annoyance over the disregard of his superior for his wishes, First Lieutenant Martin Flannery was backing away and made no attempt to help her descend. Giving a contemptuous glance and sniff, accompanied by a toss of her head which further expressed her unspoken feelings over such an exhibition of bad manners, she stepped to the ground unaided and ignored the baleful glare he directed her way.

The slender redhead found she was in front of a small and somewhat neglected-looking mansion. Although its ground floor was otherwise in darkness, light flooded through a door that was opened at the rear of the entrance hall. A figure carrying a lamp came out and approached the main entrance. Glancing to left and right, she discovered there was dense woodland in each direction. The coach prevented her from seeing what was to the rear. However, she showed no greater interest in where she might be than she had during the journey from Washington. Instead, moving aside so that Buller could pass her into the building, she turned her attention to the front door as it was opened.

Tallish, slender yet wiry, the man framed in the light of the lamp he was carrying appeared to be in his late thirties. Black hair was cropped close to his skull, and apart from a scar along his left cheek, he was swarthily handsome. Nevertheless, his pencil-line mustache tended to emphasize rather than distract from lips that suggested arrogance and cruelty. He wore a frilly-bosomed white silk shirt, opened far enough to show a hairy chest, light blue riding breeches similar to those of the two lieutenants, and brown boots with Hessian legs. His whole bearing as he crossed the porch exuded a swaggering truculence such as came to one who felt supremely confident of his ability to enforce his will upon others.

"Hello, you're earlier than I expect—!" the man greeted, his voice having the timbre of a culture that had been acquired later in life than if it had come as a result of birth and upbringing. It offered, however, no suggestion of his origins other than they were north of the Mason-Dixon line. The words came to an end as his gaze went to the beautiful young woman; then he continued, "Well now, what have we here?"

"She's with *me*!" Buller answered shortly, his intonation implying, "She's *mine,* so stay away from her!"

"I always said you had good taste, General," the man declared, striding onward with an arrogance mingled with the grace of an athlete. If he detected the meaning behind the chilling response, he ignored it and asked, "Will you present me to the young lady?"

"There's—!" Buller began, but his eyes turned from the mocking gaze directed at him. "This's Major Montreigen. He's been looking after things here for me."

"Major *Saul* Montreigen," the man elaborated, halting in front of the redhead and ignoring the glowering general.

"Enchantée, M'sieur le Majeur," Françoise answered, show-

ing no sign of noticing the right hand extended in her direction, her manner that of merely making a conventional response to a person she considered of little importance.

"Enchanté de faire votre connaisance, mademoiselle," the scar-faced man said with bad grace, allowing the proffered hand to fall to his side and continuing to speak in the same language. "Or should I say *'madame'*?"

"M'sieur le Majeur speaks the French?" Françoise inquired, reverting to her heavily accented English, without confirming her unmarried status.

"Very well, *mademoiselle,*" Montreigen boasted, running his gaze over the redhead in a speculative fashion and still speaking French. "I learned while I was running a *salle des armes* in New Orleans before the war. Is that where you come from?"

"But no, *m'sieur,*" Françoise denied. "I am from Sault Sainte Marie, in Ontario, Canada, and this is as far into the United States as I have been. You will excuse me for continuing to speak the English, but as I hope to stay in your country I wish to learn to speak it much better."

"You speak it pretty good right now, Frenchie," Buller praised, delighted by the way in which his companion was treating his scar-faced subordinate. "Is everything ready for me to see?"

"Aaranovitch went to get things ready for you when we saw the coach," Montreigen replied, the question having been directed at him. "I've seen what it does, so I'll stay and keep the young lady comp—!"

"I'm taking her with me!" the general asserted. "But there's no need for you three to come. Let's go take a look, Frenchie."

"It's no sight for a woman!" the major protested.

"She's said she wants to see what's doing and that's good enough for me," Buller answered, too aware of the other's ability as a womanizer to consider leaving the redhead behind. "Take these two for a drink while you're waiting, Montreigen. Come on, Frenchie, the sooner we've seen what's doing, the sooner we can go to—*dinner.*"

"Where'd he find her?" the major asked, his tone harsh, after the general had taken the redhead by the arm in a proprietorial fashion and led her into the mansion.

"That madam, Mrs. Cutler, fetched her and another tail-peddler to Wigg's party," Flannery answered, showing an even greater resentment over the cavalier treatment to which they had been subjected by their superior.

"Did she, by God?" Montreigen said. "I wouldn't have thought Wigg would even have known Amy Cutler, much less hired some of her girls to happy things up."

"Not some, only two," corrected the first lieutenant and explained what had happened.

"Damn my luck, I'd have liked to see the hot-assed Mary Wilkinson having the shit beat out of her," the major growled, at the conclusion of the description, then nodded after the departing couple. "Why's he taking her to see what Aaranovitch's got for him, though?"

"Don't ask *me* what goes on in that uncouth bastard's mind!" Flannery snapped indignantly. "Bobbie and I tried to talk him out of bringing her with us, but you know what he's like."

"Better than either of you, it looks like," Montreigen stated dryly. "You've both been around him long enough to know better than let him see you're against anything he says he's going to do. That only makes him all the more goddamned bull-headed set on doing it, just to prove he's the Big Boss. I suppose he's figuring on taking her back to Arkansas to fight other women for him?"

"That could be what he's got in mind, him finding it so goddamned amusing and horn-raising to watch," Flannery conceded grudgingly, despite realizing that the major was correct in his assessment of the way their superior invariably reacted to opposition to his intentions. "He asked her to come with us at Wigg's as soon as she told him how much she liked fighting, but we couldn't hear what they said to each other in the coach on the way here."

"He asked her to go to Arkansas?" the major queried.

"No, just to have *dinner* with him when he was through," Flannery corrected. "And we know what *that* means."

"Sure," Montreigen grunted. "He wouldn't ask her to go off with him while Amy Cutler was listening. She wouldn't take kind to losing a girl that good. Only, when he asked her, she could have fought shy on account of how badly things are going for him in Arkansas. That being so, he's showing her that he's got something to turn the tables on the Rebs."

"Why should he go to all that trouble?" Second Lieutenant Robert Cryer inquired. "He's never had any difficulty getting women to fight for him out there."

"That's true," Montreigen admitted. "Only they all look like what they are."

"How do you mean?" Flannery asked.

"Like I said, everything about them shows what they are," the major answered and, seeing neither lieutenant showed signs of enlightenment, elaborated, "They're either cheap whores, or poor white trash, fighting because they need the money."

"She's only a whore herself," Cryer exclaimed. "If she wasn't, she wouldn't have been with Mrs. Cutler."

"That's as may be," Montreigen replied, with the kind of patience frequently shown when explaining a point which should be obvious. "But, get her dressed right, talking and acting the way she does, and she'd pass as one of the guests. The way she acted when he introduced us put me in mind of those nose-in-the-air, high-and-mighty 'old family' French-Creole gals I came across while I was in New Orleans."

"She said she'd never been there," Cryer pointed out sulkily, glancing to where the couple under discussion had disappeared, through the door at the far side of the entrance hall.

"I'm not saying she *has*," the major countered. "All I said was, she put me in mind of those high-toned Creoles. Neither the gal she was put up against or the fellers watching would expect her to be able to fight as good as you reckon she can, and Buller could make a killing betting on her."

"But *we* know about her," Cryer reminded.

"And he'll warn you to keep quiet," Montreigen stated.

"What is it that Aaranovitch has come up with?" Flannery asked, deciding against mentioning certain speculations aroused by the conversation as he wanted to keep all the credit to himself should they prove correct.

"It's everything he said it would be and will do all Buller wants," Flannery assessed, after describing an experiment he had witnessed. Then he nodded towards the closed door and concluded, "One thing's for sure. That redheaded gal's going to wish she'd stayed out here with us. When you see the son of a bitch working, that stuff concocted by Aaranovitch is like to turn your stomach."

"Good evening, Mist—*General* Buller!" David Aaranovitch greeted, rising from the rocking chair he had been occupying and peering through spectacles with strong lenses intended for reading or working at close quarters. Removing them, he blinked a couple of times at the newcomers as if unable to believe what he was seeing. Then he continued in his high-pitched New England accent, "What is *she* doing here?"

Of slightly less than medium height, scrawny, narrow-chested, and round-shouldered, the speaker was far from an imposing physical specimen. Under an untidy mop of frizzy mousy-brown hair, having an overlarge nose, bulging eyes, and a badly shaved receding chin, his pallid and pimply features were thin. He was wearing a grubby and much-stained long white coat, which hung open to display an equally dirty collarless white shirt and yellowish-brown Nankeen trousers with legs so long they almost obscured the toes of his badly scuffed and apparently never cleaned black boots.

"I've brought her to see what you've done for me," Buller answered, glancing around. "So I hope it's as good as your letter made it out to be."

Formerly the main kitchen for the mansion, the sizable room had been converted into a well-equipped scientific laboratory. The most noticeable objects, standing on a long and sturdy bench that had originally been used for preparing food, were three of the very large glass bottles known as carboys. They had been removed from the wooden or wicker containers that were employed to offer greater safety when in use for transporting acid or other corrosive fluids in quantity. Two were empty and open, their glass stoppers being alongside them, but the other had a deep layer of soil in it and was closed. Nearby, in cages, were half a dozen brown rats.

"It is, I can assure you of that," Aaranovitch declared. "But I hardly think the young lady should be here while I demonstrate."

"Is it that dangerous?" Buller demanded, glaring about him with obvious consternation.

"Not so much *dangerous* as most unpleasant to watch," the chemist corrected, smiling in a superior fashion. "There's nothing for you to be afraid of."

"Afraid!" the general barked and, as was his instinctive reaction in times of stress, took out his bulky silver cigar case. "I'm not *afraid,* damn it. What do you say, Frenchie, are you game to see what's doing?"

"That is why I came, *M'sieur le* General," Françoise replied. "And, as you will find out, I *never* go back on anything I say I will do."

"Which I'm counting on you to prove later," Buller asserted, eyeing the redhead in a knowing manner. Opening the case, he took out a thick cigar as he went on, "All right, young feller, let's be seeing what you've been spending so much of my money on."

"Very well," Aaranovitch assented, his air of superiority being replaced by petulance. He looked around as he was speaking and his voice took on a note of warning as he saw what his sponsor was holding. "Don't light that cigar until after I've finished. The compound is highly combustible."

"Combusti—!" Buller began, refraining from reaching into his trousers pocket for matches.

"That means it catches fire easily," the chemist explained.

"I know what the son of a bitch means!" the general snarled irritably, replacing the cigar and returning the case. "Just what the hell is it you've come up with?"

"What you asked me for," Aaranovitch replied. "Something that will give your troops an ascendancy over the weapons and fighting skills of the Rebels they are up against."

"I should goddamned hope it *will*!" Buller growled, waving his right hand in a gesture that encompassed all the paraphernalia in the room. "I've paid out enough money for you to do the son of a bitch for me."

"The results more than justify your expenditure," Aaranovitch claimed, his thin features showing annoyance. "In fact, what I have discovered will prove so effective that, once it becomes known, no nation will dare go to war against another in case it should be used against them."

"How do you mean?" the general demanded. " 'When it becomes known'!"

"You can hardly keep its use a secret," the chemist pointed out. "And after you've shown how effective it is, every military nation will be clamoring to buy the formula and make it."

"You can leave that side of it to *me*!" Buller ordered, then went on with an impatient eagerness, "Let's see what it is and does."

"Certainly," Aaranovitch replied. Crossing to the safe in a corner of the room, he unlocked and opened the door. Reaching inside, he turned, holding a bottle containing a yellowish-brown liquid. "I began by trying to produce the kind of virulently toxic compound you wanted to poison the rivers, lakes, and wells used by the Rebels, but decided this offered a far more practical solution."

"What is it?" Buller asked, piggy eyes glinting avariciously.

"A mixture of dichloro—!" the chemist commenced, but his thin face took on a cunning expression. "I think it is best that I keep the formula to myself for the time being, as—*insurance,* shall we say?"

"Why you—!" the general spat out, his porcine features darkening with anger. Realizing he was in no position to adopt too high-handed an attitude, he halted his words and, giving a shrug, forced a humorless grin and went on in a milder tone,

"All right, I suppose I can't blame you for playing it cagey. I just hope that stuff is as good as you reckon."

"You will soon be able to judge that for yourself," Aaranovitch stated smugly.

Going to the work bench, the chemist removed the glass stopper from the bottle and tipped some of the liquid into one of the open carboys. Almost immediately, a yellow vapor began to form. Having "corked" the bottle as soon as he stopped pouring, he set it aside to take up and don a pair of thick leather gloves. Opening a cage, he reached for and caught the rat it held. Dragging the squealing and wildly struggling animal out, he managed after a couple of tries to thrust its head into the neck of the carboy and shoved it onward.

Falling to the bottom of the transparent vessel on being released, the rat contrived to land on its feet. Following the dictates of its instinct, it started to run through the evaporating liquid. Almost immediately, it gave a screech of pain and bounded into the air as if stung or finding the surface it was crossing too hot to bear. On alighting, it toppled and its feet pawed at its eyes. Rolling and thrashing around, its shrieks became what in a human being would have been a strangled coughing. After a few seconds of what was obviously tremendous torment, the violent convulsions ended and it subsided into the still-growing cloud of vapor. In addition to the pads of its feet being red and raw-looking, several severe blisters had formed on the bare flesh of its belly and tail.

"As you can see," Aaranovitch was saying while the events were taking place, speaking with the calm detachment of a lecturer addressing students in a classroom, "in addition to giving off toxic gases when exposed to the air, the fluid causes severe burning with destruction of the tissue with which it comes in contact. Its power of penetration of the skin is very considerable due to its capability of producing lipoid solubility. As a result of its action, the vapor creates a strong irritant effect on the eyes, lungs, and skin. Furthermore—!"

"Good God Almighty!" Buller ejaculated profanely, having

been staring so intently at the carboy he had paid no attention to the comments by the chemist. "Did you see *that*, Frenchie?"

"Yes!" the redhead replied, her face set in lines of loathing.

"You haven't seen it all," Aaranovitch stated, pointing along the bench. "The effects of the fluid and its vapor are lingering and not easily destroyed by weathering. I poured some on the soil in that carboy six days ago. Watch what happens."

Collecting another rat, the chemist removed the stopper from the carboy and thrust it in. Falling to the soil without injury, it soon exhibited similar symptoms of distress to those of the first animal. Its suffering was more prolonged before it too succumbed.

"Well?" Aaranovitch inquired triumphantly, replacing the glass stopper.

"You've done the son of a bitch!" Buller enthused, rubbing his hands together in delight. *"This* will win the war for me. Frenchie, you can come to Arkansas now and know you'll be safe."

"Perhaps, *M'sieur le* General," Françoise answered, showing less enthusiasm and clearly making an effort to conceal the revulsion she was experiencing. She turned her gaze from the gruesome contents of the carboys. "But how are you going to be able to put the Rebel soldiers into such bottles?"

6

I Should Kill You

"Welcome to my-sh humble abo—abodsh, Frenchie-gal!" Brigadier General Moses J. Buller announced, with the solemnity of one who had drunk not wisely but too well. Needing to brace himself still further against the slender redhead, who had taken over the task of guiding and supporting him from Lieutenants Martin Flannery and Robert Cryer, he kicked the door closed in their faces. "Let'sh you 'n' me get undresh—under-esheded —get our clo-eshes off quick, so's I can find out if you-sh ash good in bed-sh as you are-sh at fighting."

"You will not be disappointed, *mon cher* General," Françoise promised, showing no such signs of intoxication. Slipping from the grasp of the burly officer, she made for the dressing table and continued, "But first, although as I have told you, I do not usually drink the hard liquor, let me join you in our own private toast to the gas that burns like the acid and will bring you the victory in Arkansas."

"S-Sure, let'sh do that!" Buller authorized, reeling on far

from steady legs to collapse rather than sit on the bed. "You pour-sh the son of a bitch out 'n' you 'n' me'sh'll drink her down. Only don't go taking too long-sh to be doing it, Frenchie-gal. I'm all-sh hot 'n' ready for what you'sh been promising me all-sh night!"

Although he had been most impressed by what he had seen in the laboratory, the comment made by the redhead had served to warn the general that he might be premature in believing his military problems were solved. Therefore, instead of having accepted the demonstration as conclusive proof, he had sought enlightenment on the point she had raised. What he had heard was satisfactory. According to David Aaranovitch, there would be no great difficulty in employing the liquid and the resultant gases against the Confederate soldiers. This could be done either by means of the kind of artillery shell used to deliver incendiary compounds, or by allowing the gases to be blown to them on the wind. In the latter case, the chemist had asserted, this could be done without danger to the dispatchers provided the precautions he outlined were adhered to.

Prompted further by the redhead, who had claimed her sole interest was in ascertaining whether it would be safe for her to accompany him to Arkansas, Buller had asked whether an adequate supply of the fluid could be prepared in the vicinity of his headquarters. He was assured by Aaranovitch that, in addition to four carboys made ready for use, the ingredients for more were available and all the equipment required to mix them had been obtained. In fact, the chemist had stated, it was possible to leave and recommence manufacture the following morning if necessary. On being asked if she was satisfied, Françoise had said she was and would now be willing to accept the offer of sponsorship made by the general.

Delighted by having discovered that both aspects of his affairs were apparently progressing in the manner he desired, Buller had announced he was in the mood for a celebration. Nor had he been willing to wait until returning to his hotel in Washington. Instead, accompanied by Françoise and Aaranovitch, he had returned to the entrance hall of the mansion.

Finding it empty, he had been led by the chemist to the comfortably furnished quarters of Major Saul Montreigen on the second floor. Finding his two lieutenants there, he had demanded rather than requested liquor to toast the result of Aaranovitch's efforts, making what he had clearly considered the witty comment that he did not doubt the liquor had been purchased with his money. Nor, such was the state of his exhilaration, had he raised any objections when the redhead declined to drink on the grounds that doing so had an adverse effect upon her physical condition. Praising her desire to keep in trim, he had not shown a similar abstinence.

After having darted a lascivious glance at Françoise, Montreigen had set about getting his superior drunk in the hope of producing a stupor that would leave her unattended for the night. It seemed that the ploy would succeed, Buller soon proving to be unable to hold his liquor. What was more, due to his ebullient frame of mind, the whiskey he had consumed did not arouse the truculence his subordinates had seen it produce on previous occasions. Instead, he had described the display he had seen in the former kitchen and had grown heavily jocular with the lieutenants over his having saved them from watching the gruesome end of the rats.

Unfortunately for the major, his designs upon the redhead failed to materialize. Giving no indication of suspecting what he had in mind, she had remarked pointedly to the general that she had been promised "dinner" and was ready to indulge in it. Taking the hint, Buller had announced they would be leaving. He had also given orders for Montreigen to make everything ready to set out for Arkansas by noon the following day. Then, carrying along an unopened bottle of whiskey, he had escorted her to the waiting Concord coach. Ordering the same mode of travel, he and she had gone inside while the lieutenants rode on the box.

Once again respecting the disinclination of the slender girl to be the recipient of his attentions until they arrived at their destination, the general had instead contrived to empty the bottle during the return journey. Such was his state of intoxication, he had required the assistance of the lieutenants to ascend to the third floor of the luxurious hotel. It said much for the sturdy condition of the building that, despite the hour being well past midnight, the noise he made had not disturbed anybody while this had been taking place. On reaching his suite, he had told the pair that he could manage. Leaving them to go to the second bedroom they were sharing, and assisted by Françoise, he entered his own sleeping quarters.

On reaching the dressing table, the redhead placed her parasol and reticule on it. Without removing her hat or turning the light of the lamp hanging from a hook above it any higher, she removed the stopper from a crystal decanter on a tray. A sniff informed her the contents were brandy. Glancing over her shoulder to where the general sat swaying on the edge of the bed and fumbling at the buttons of his tunic, she poured a generous quantity into the glasses, which were also supplied by the hotel. However, she did not turn immediately. Instead, her right forefinger pressed at the side of the bulky gold ring she wore on her left hand. The top flipped up to reveal a cavity from which she poured the white powder it held into one of the glasses. Closing the cover of the ring, she shook the glass gently until the additive had dissolved without in any way leaving evidence of its presence in the liquor.

"Here you are, *mon cher* General," Françoise said, crossing to the bed and offering the glass to which she had added the powder. "To the success you deserve!"

"T-To the shuck-shess I desh-erve!" Buller repeated, grasping the glass and peering at it owlishly.

"Such a toast must be drunk to the very bottom of the glass," the redhead asserted and made as if to carry out her instructions.

Nodding and using both hands to do so, the general raised and tilted the entire contents into his mouth. Gagging and spitting some of it out, he nevertheless contrived to send the greater part down his throat. Then, throwing the glass aside, he once more began to fumble at the buttons. His mouth slobbered, making what were supposed to be profanities, as he found his fingers were failing to obey the dictates of his mind. Snarling with rage, he made as if to rise.

"Let me help!" Françoise offered, throwing the contents of her glass onto the floor and setting it upon the bedside table.

Although it was unlikely the general understood what was said, he made no attempt to resist as the redhead reached for the front of his tunic. Instead, he began to sway forward and his head flopped involuntarily from side to side. Shoving him backward across the bed, where he sprawled breathing stentoriously, she straightened and looked down with an expression of loathing.

"I should kill you for what you're planning to do!" the beautiful young woman hissed, picking up a pillow and holding it over the porcine face of the burly man. "It would be so *easy* and I'd like nothing better after what I saw tonight, but that isn't the way to do what needs doing!"

Buller would never know how close he had been to death at that moment.

The words were spoken with heartfelt bitterness, but no longer after the fashion of a person employing a language other than that of her birth.

Instead, the voice was that of a well-educated Southron.

Montreigen had been closer to the truth than he realized when asking if the girl who had been introduced as "Françoise, from Sault Sainte Marie, Ontario, Canada" was from New Orleans. While this was not the case, she had been born and raised in Louisiana and frequently visited that city before the war. Her name was Belle Boyd, and seeking vengeance upon the men who caused the murder of her parents, she had acquired such fame as a member of the Confederate Secret Service that she had been awarded the sobriquet "the Rebel Spy" among friends and foes alike.

Delivering dispatches to Mrs. Amy Cutler, who operated an efficient spy ring based in Washington, Belle had been asked for assistance. Although it was generally accepted by the authorities that Aaranovitch was trying to create a new system of preserving foodstuffs under the sponsorship of Buller, whose

fortune was made by producing such commodities, the madam
had been suspicious. However, she had so far failed to satisfy
her curiosity. So excellent was the system of guarding developed by Montreigen, she had been unable to have an examination of the mansion carried out. Nor had any of the soldiers
employed there known more than that some kind of "scientifi-
cal" experimentation was being performed by the chemist.

Learning that the general was on his way to the capital,
ostensibly for discussion with his superiors, Mrs. Cutler had
deduced the experiments had been concluded successfully.
Knowing of his hobby of watching women fight, and having
been told of the dinner party to which he was to be invited, she
had decided his erotic taste in entertainment could be made to
serve her purpose. Arranging for George Wigg to be told how
he might best ingratiate himself with Buller, she had been asked
to supply the means. Lotte was a frequent contender in such
events, although not a member of the spy ring and unaware of
its existence. Therefore, knowing of Belle's ability at *savate* and
other forms of unarmed combat, the madam had suggested she
act as opponent for the blonde. Accepting the proposition, the
Rebel Spy had dyed her always short-cropped black hair to the
violent shade of red and stained her skin to the appropriate hue
to become the French-Canadian Françoise.

As originally envisaged, wishing to avoid the chance of her
sustaining injuries that would reduce her ability to defend herself should anything go wrong, Belle was merely to make a
pretense of fighting with Lotte. Having done so on previous
occasions, the blonde would not have been suspicious about
such instructions. When the bout had ended, with her as the
"loser," the "redhead" would then have complained to Buller
that she was under orders that had precluded her doing her
utmost and winning. Then, employing her considerable histri-
onic ability, she was to try and win his confidence by stressing
her alleged enjoyment of engaging in serious combat against
members of her sex. On learning of this, it had been hoped he
would extend an invitation for her to accompany him to Arkansas.

Circumstances had offered another way of bringing about the invitation.

On arriving at the mansion, Mrs. Cutler had been informed that Mary Wilkinson was present as a guest. Mrs. Cutler had taken advantage of Lotte's being absent to answer the call of nature and alerted Belle to her background and attitudes. Neither had envisaged her participation in the way it had happened, but had decided she might issue a challenge on seeing the poor display being given by the supposedly bitter rivals. Therefore, the madam had kept a surreptitious watch on the audience. Despite having been unable to overhear what was being said, she had drawn the correct conclusions from the sight of the brunette starting to disrobe after concluding her conversation with Buller. In what had passed as a signal for her "young ladies" to give a more convincing performance, she had warned Belle of the possibility of an unannounced intervention. By suggesting they should get to their feet, Belle had been ready to defend herself when the attack by the brunette was launched. While she would have preferred to deal with Mary unaided and had taken the earliest opportunity with which she was presented to render the blonde *hors de combat,* remembering what she had been told, she had felt not the slightest compunction over the punishment she had inflicted upon the brunette. She had drawn consolation by knowing Lotte would be well compensated for the way in which the affair had turned out.

Granted the opportunity to exhibit her skill, instead of merely having to imply its existence verbally, Belle had succeeded in arousing the interest of the general. Then, reverting to the original plan, she had persuaded him to let her join him in seeing the result of the work carried out by Aaranovitch. However, regardless of the way in which she had flaunted her half-naked body before his lascivious gaze at the conclusion of the fight, she had had no intention of allowing him to achieve his intentions so far as she was concerned when they reached the hotel. She had been prepared to prevent this happening, and

was assisted by the way he had behaved in his delight over what
he had seen and learned about the use of the liquid.

Tossing aside the pillow with a gesture redolent of regret,
Belle glanced around the room. Secure in the knowledge that it
would be several hours before Buller recovered from the effects
of the opiate she had administered, she decided to find out if he
was carrying or had with him any documents which might be
of use to the Confederate Secret Service and High Command.
Apart from a thick wad of bank notes, which she made no
attempt to remove, his wallet held nothing. Returning it to the
inside pocket of his tunic, she went to check the contents of the
dressing table's drawers. These yielded only a bulky leather
dispatch case, the fastening strap of which was locked. Raising
the hem of her skirt, she pulled from its place of concealment in
the leg of the right high-buttoned shoe a small piece of metal
shaped like a modern golfer's iron. A few manipulations with
the curved head of the device caused the lock's mechanism to
operate and freed the strap. However, on examination of the
documents, she discovered they were concerned with routine
matters of no special significance.

Closing and relocking the case, Belle replaced it and continued her search. Satisfied that her efforts were not worthwhile,
she returned the lock pick to its hiding place and went to the
bed. Showing her repugnance of the task, she removed Buller's
boots and pungently smelling socks. Raising his no more aro-
matic bare feet onto the quilt, she laid him comfortably. Then,
collecting the reticule and parasol, she went to the second of
the room's doors. Unlocking and opening it, she closed it behind her and walked along the dimly lit passage toward the
stairs leading to the lower floors.

Setting off to rendezvous with a waiting member of the spy
ring and tell of her discovery, the Rebel Spy thought with satisfaction of how she had been helped in her assignment by Buller's choice of temporary accommodation. Being aware that
many of the clientele might wish secrecy in the comings and
goings from their rooms, particularly during the night, the hotel had built up a well-deserved reputation for the privacy it

offered. Not only were the rooms practically soundproof, the thick carpets allowed guests to arrive or leave with little noise. A further aid to this was provided by having the locks and hinges of every door kept well oiled to eliminate squeaking. Although there was a small staff available from midnight, they remained in the kitchen at the rear and only went upstairs in response to a signal from the bell with which each room was equipped.

Even as Belle was drawing her conclusions, she learned the efforts at securing privacy for the guests also had disadvantages.

Continuing to refrain from mentioning his suspicions, being unwilling to share any praise if they should prove correct and feeling sure Cryer would report him to Buller as a means of gaining approval in the event of his being wrong, Flannery had made preparations to keep the "redhead" under surveillance. Removing his *colpack* busby hat, dolman jacket, and boots on entering the second bedroom, he had waited a few minutes without undressing any further until his companion had fallen asleep. Then he had reached and looked through the keyhole of the sitting room's connecting door while "Françoise" was picking the lock on the dispatch case.

Wanting to be able to present as strong a case as possible, realizing his superior would be far from pleased to hear what had happened, Flannery had allowed his intended victim to go into the passage instead of entering and capturing her by the bed. Then, taking advantage of the well-oiled hinges, he left the suite by the door of the sitting room. Following silently across the thick carpet which—unbeknown to him—the girl was admiring for its sound-muffling qualities, he had decided how he would deal with her. The method he had selected was to offer even greater benefits than he envisaged.

Coming into range without his presence being detected, Flannery caught Belle by the right wrist and bicep to twist the arm behind her back in a hammerlock. Taken with the pain of the hold, surprise caused her to drop her parasol and reticule. Apart from containing a piece of possibly incriminating evi-

dence, in the form of a key for Mrs. Cutler's private entrance to
the brothel, the loss of the latter was of no special consequence.
However, having a powerful spring-loaded billy telescoped in
the detachable handle, the former would have offered her a
readily accessible weapon. What was more, the way in which
she was grasped prevented her from employing another protective device she had on her person.

"Where do you think you're going?" Flannery demanded,
bringing his captive to a halt.

"I—I am searching for the—lavatory, do you call it?" Belle
answered, retaining sufficient presence of mind to employ her
"Françoise" manner of speaking.

"There's a chamberpot under the bed," the lieutenant
pointed out.

"Oui, m'sieur," the "redhead" conceded. "But I thought
M'sieur le General would need to vomit when he wakes up and
would not wish to put his face close to the shit to do it."

"I *might* have believed you if I hadn't seen you going
through his dispatch case," Flannery claimed. "As it is, I'm
going to take you into the basement and make you talk!"

With that, the lieutenant gave a push intended to start the
girl moving. Giving a gasp, she let her body relax and leaned
backward. Shifting her weight onto the right foot while doing
so, she swung her left arm upward. Passing it rapidly around
his right arm, she caught hold of his left wrist with her hand. A
startled exclamation burst from him as he found his arms
locked. Swinging her left leg in front of his, she pivoted her
slender body to the right and, by applying pressure on his right
arm, caused him to flip over in a half somersault.

Despite having freed herself, Belle discovered another disadvantage of the thick carpet. Flannery was taken unawares by
her tactics, but his skill at wrestling helped him reduce the
impact as he came down upon the yielding surface. What was
more, he proved able to react with disconcerting rapidity when
she tried to continue her attack. Catching her right ankle as she
launched a kick toward his head, he gave her a shove of such
force it sent her reeling to crash into the wall. Leaping up

swiftly, he lunged to grasp the front of her blouse before she was able to prevent it and drew back his other fist for a punch.

Although unable to avoid being caught, Belle was far from helpless, as the loss of the parasol had not left her completely unarmed. Shaking down the broad metal bracelet, she gripped it and swung her right arm in a chopping motion an instant before Flannery could strike at her. The edge that caught his face was very sharp and gashed open his cheek. Snarling in a mixture of rage and pain, he heaved with such force she was once more flung away from him. However, she had regained sufficient control over her movements by the time she reached the end of the passage to stop just clear of the window.

Turning, Belle found the lieutenant already coming toward her. In his anger, which had increased by having touched his gashed face and realizing he would be scarred for life, he was making his attack after the fashion of a rage-blinded fighting bull charging a *matador*. Stepping aside at the last moment, she avoided his reaching hands and snapped a kick to his groin. The furious curses he was uttering changed to a croak of torment. He began to fold at the waist, but was not halted. Instead, he rammed headfirst into the window. Sash and glass shattered as he went through to fall to the hard-packed ground of what a later generation would refer to as a parking lot.

"Damn it!" Belle breathed, turning to hurry along the passage without offering to look outside and ascertain how badly her attacker was hurt, although sure he would be in no condition to interrupt her departure. "I'll never be able to explain away what happened, so I won't be able to stay around Buller!"

Retrieving her reticule and parasol, the Rebel Spy drew consolation from the thought that she had at least discovered the nature of the terrible liquid which the general intended to employ against the Confederate troops in Arkansas. Furthermore, she had retained her liberty and, while it was unlikely she could regain the general's confidence, she would be able to help seek out a means to counter the terrible threat the liquid posed.

7

It's the Rebs!

"They'll do!" Major Gerald Buller asserted, his manner disinterested, at the conclusion of a perfunctory inspection of the two ranks of soldiers standing alongside their saddled horses. "Mount them up and we'll get going!"

"Excuse me, sir!" First Lieutenant Kirby Cogshill replied, instead of giving the appropriate order. "Our relief isn't even in sight yet."

"That's their fault, not mine!" Buller claimed and swung onto the saddle of his fine bay gelding with the skill acquired hunting foxes back east. "We finished our duty here at daybreak, which's well past, so we're going!"

"But the bridge, *sir*—!" Cogshill began, indicating the object to which he was referring with a gesture of his right hand and refraining from mounting his equally spirited brown horse.

Apart from being around six feet in height and having the same badges on their headdress, there was little in their attire to

suggest the speakers were both members of the New Hampstead Volunteers Company A.

Handsome, except for his features starting to show the
ravages of dissipation, Buller resembled his elder brother in
that he was bulky and running to fat. Except for his headdress,
from beneath which showed longish black hair, his attire was of
the same style worn by Lieutenants Martin Flannery and Robert Cryer. Brimless and with its crown, decorated by a gold
tassel, extending to dangle almost to neck level at the right side,
the exception was based upon the less elaborate *bonnet de police*
undress cap of an officer in the *Chasseurs à Cheval* of the
French Imperial Guard, upon which their elaborate uniform
was based. Suspended on the slings at the left side of his
weapon belt was a saber curved in the fashion of a Persian
scimitar, and butt-forward in the closed top holster on the right
rode a Tiffany-handled Colt Model of 1855 Navy revolver.

More slender and clearly much fitter, at twenty-one, Cogshill
was some ten years younger than his superior. He kept his light
brown hair shorter, and his freckled, good-looking face expressed a greater strength of character. Born into a family that
had provided competent officers for the Army of the United
States since the War of Independence against Great—as it was
then—Britain, he had won his commission via attendance at
the military academy at West Point. Despite having been sent
to serve with a regiment of volunteers, his uniform was of the
vastly more utilitarian pattern prescribed by the *Manuel of
Dress Regulations.* While having been purchased privately, his
saddle, Colt 1860 Army revolver, saber, and the rig upon which
the last two were carried also all conformed to the rules governing such items.

"What's wrong with it?" Buller challenged, his manner redolent of irony, watching the reaction of the enlisted men to his
wit. "It looks fine to *me.* How about you, Mr. Packard?"

"I've never seen a better built 'n' anywheres in this whole
goddamned Toothpick State, Major," replied the man to whom
the question was directed, also making no attempt to look at
the bridge. "And, 'less I miss my guess, ain't none of them

stinkin' Johnny Rebs come round in the night and snuck it away."

Not quite as tall as the officers, Sergeant Major Alden Packard was thickset and muscular. His brutal face had a broken nose and other indications that he had fought in the bare-knuckle boxing bouts that were still popular, but he had had sufficient sense to quit before his wits suffered permanent damage. Like Cogshill and the enlisted men, he was dressed and equipped in the fashion of the regular army. Although his uniform was strained at the seams by his bulk, it was all hard flesh. Prior to having accompanied the Bullers into their regiment, he had been employed as a foreman who could enforce the will of the elder brother upon their employees. As in civilian life, although he had hoped for the pay and privileges of an officer, he held his present rank more by virtue of his fistic prowess than other qualifications.

"It's not real *likely* the gutless bastards would even try by night and even less by day," Buller claimed. "Or maybe you're forgetting we've run them clear across the Ouachita River, and that's a good thirty miles from here?"

"Mount up!" Packard bellowed, before Cogshill—to whom the mocking question was addressed—could reply. "We're pulling out!"

Watching the order being carried out with alacrity, but none of the orderly skill of well-trained cavalry soldiers, Cogshill was annoyed and concerned. Nor was the former emotion caused by what he knew to be a deliberate attempt to undermine his authority with the enlisted men. Being a professional soldier, albeit as yet unblooded in combat, he knew the strategic value of the bridge under discussion. Running down the northern slope of the Mushogen Valley, the Old Corn Road passed over it and ascended the southern incline. It offered the only place in many miles at which heavy traffic could cross the wide and swiftly flowing Mushogen River. To the untrained eye, it looked easy to defend and, the lieutenant was willing to admit, this was the case providing sensible precautions were taken. Apart from a few clumps of flowering dogwood bushes, which the guard would have searched if they had not been ordered to parade for inspection by their commanding officer, the terrain was open on each side as far as the skyline.

Having been well trained for his work, Cogshill was worried about the lax way in which the guard duty was being performed. He did not underestimate the skill and courage of the enemy. While the Confederate Army of Arkansas and North Texas were beyond the Ouachita River, they had withdrawn there in an orderly fashion rather than being "run" before the arrival of the Bullers. Furthermore, they were showing no signs of continuing their retreat. Instead, they were standing their ground, and their very efficient cavalry constantly raided the Union forces, causing a steady drain of men and material by their efforts. They had, in fact, frequently struck even farther north than the "good thirty miles" they had retired; which was the reason the predecessor of Brigadier General Moses J. Buller had insisted upon a guard being mounted to protect the bridge.

"Well, *Mr.* Cogshill," the major growled, swinging onto the back of his bay. "Are you coming with us or staying here?"

"Yo!" the lieutenant answered, his tone flat and showing no emotion.

Even if his training at West Point had not stressed that officers should not air differences of opinion in the hearing of enlisted men, Cogshill was too wise to make more than the traditional response and mount his fine-looking blaze-faced bay gelding. He was aware that Buller longed for an opportunity to have him and the other few regular officers removed from the regiment. While another professional could have achieved this in a number of ways, the major lacked the requisite military knowledge. For all that, the lieutenant had no intention of paving the way for a charge of either insubordination or disobedience of orders to be laid against him.

While the conversation was taking place, one of the enlisted men had looked past the officers and sergeant major. Glancing idly up the southern rim, he noticed a number of mounted men appearing on it. Being a green rookie, his first thought was that the relief guard was approaching. Then he realized this was incorrect. In the first place, the newcomers formed a single line along the rim instead of appearing in a double file. Secondly, even at the distance separating him from them, he saw that the uniforms they wore were not of the dark blue which practically all the Union Army were now wearing. Rather, the color was a yellowish-gray, which he remembered having heard described as butternut.

Almost twenty seconds went by before the implication of the color struck the volunteer.

"Up there!" the enlisted man yelled, his voice squeaky with excitement and alarm. "It's the Rebs!"

Instantly, as they turned their horses in the direction indicated by the volunteer, the difference between Buller and Cogshill became obvious. After taking in the sight, while his superior did nothing more than stare up the slope, the lieutenant prepared to give orders the moment he discovered the intentions of the men on the rim. For his part, a cold chill of anxiety hit the major as he realized he was for the first time confronted by some of the "Johnny Reb scum" he had frequently boasted he would rout in battle. He found the prospect more disconcerting, almost frightening, than exhilarating.

Seeing he and his men were observed, the tall young officer in the center of the rank swept off his white campaign hat to show fiery red hair and a freckled, pugnaciously handsome face. Waving the headdress in a forward motion, he shouted a single word. However, it needed no more. Showing a discipline and riding skill far beyond that of the Volunteers, the gray-clad newcomers started to ride down the slope. Watching them, Cogshill began to have grave doubts over the ability of his men to hold the bridge. Not only did the Rebels appear to be veterans, but the weapons they drew were mostly Colt 1860 Army revolvers, arguably the finest handguns yet made. Against them, the guard had to depend upon much cheaper Pettingill, Joslyn, Manhattan, or Metropolitan revolvers, and had in addition received far too little training in their use.

Even as the lieutenant was forming his far from palatable conclusions, Buller took matters from his hands.

"Get them!" the major howled, hauling his ornate Navy Colt from its holster. "Shoot the bastards down!"

"Move yourselves, damn you!" Packard supplemented, liberating his Manhattan Navy revolver.

Following the example of their superiors, the enlisted men armed themselves. Then, although the attackers were still beyond the range at which anything other than a very lucky hit might be expected, they all fired. Alarm bit into Cogshill as he saw the difficulty the men started to have in controlling the horses. However, it appeared their aggressive actions had paid off. In the wake of the shots, the Rebels—none of whom had been hit—made rapid turns and rode in the direction from which they had come. The lieutenant could hardly believe his eyes. However, the major decided his theories about the cowardice of the Confederate soldiers were true.

"After them!" Buller bellowed, setting spurs to his mount and waving his smoking revolver as it set off. "We'll massacre the bastards!"

Remembering a lecture on the tactics employed by Indians, Cogshill was not allowed to mention it. Inspired by the example of their commanding officer, the enlisted men followed him in more of a wild rush than a disciplined charge. Watching them go by, the lieutenant was torn between two conflicting duties: to accompany his company and try to bring order to its members, or remain and guard the bridge. Deciding the former might be the wiser course, as he could form a more accurate idea of what was going on, he signaled for his restlessly moving mount to go after the others.

Reaching the top of the slope, filled with a growing suspicion that they were playing into the hands of the enemy—who were holding their formation remarkably well for a mob running scared—instinct caused Cogshill to look back. Immediately, he reined his horse to a halt. What he saw warned him he might disobey the orders of his superior officer and quit his company at a time when they might need the knowledge acquired during his training. It went beyond trying to save the half-trained Volunteers from the folly into which he was convinced they were being led. Aware that his conduct could be misinterpreted should anything go wrong, he swung and started his horse galloping down the slope. Before he had covered half the distance, there was a commotion from his rear. It warned him that he had been correct in his assumptions with regards to the behavior of the Rebels. For all that, despite his assessment of what was taking place, he refused to turn back.

"Blast that Yankee luff!" Sergeant Kiowa Cotton growled, more admiration than anger in his tone despite employing a derogatory name for a first lieutenant. "He's seen us and's on his way back, head down and horns a-hooking!"

"Some folks want *everything* too damned easy," replied Captain Dustine Edward Marsden ("Dusty") Fog. "And before you tell me, I'm one the same as you."

Anybody who had spent a reasonable amount of time traveling around what had once been the United States of America would have known that, although from different strata of society, the speakers were born and raised in Texas.

Tall, lean, so dark and hawk-nosed the reason for his only known given name was obvious, the sergeant looked like—and was—a dangerous man to have as an enemy, a quality acquired mainly from his maternal parentage in a mixed-race marriage. On his close-cropped black hair was a yellow-topped *kepi,* bearing a silver five-pointed-star-in-a-circle badge with a laurel wreath motif around the star, which was embossed with the letters T.L.C. A tight-rolled red bandana trailed its long ends over the front of his waist-length, double-breasted, cadet-gray tunic. Ending in the knee-high leggings of Kiowa moccasins, his yellow-striped riding breeches were encircled by a western-style gunbelt. At the left side, butt forward for a cross draw, was holstered a Remington 1861 Army revolver, and the sheath at the right carried a massive bowie knife. As his hands were otherwise filled, he was carrying a Henry repeating rifle suspended by its sling across his shoulders.

Despite having won promotion to captain in the field, and being given command of the Texas Light Cavalry's hard-riding,

harder-fighting Company C, Dusty Fog was not yet eighteen.
Standing not more than five feet six in his black Jefferson boots,
there was something about him that explained how he had
earned his rapid ascent to that rank and how he had already
acquired something close to legendary status in Arkansas.
There was a width to his shoulders, tapering to a slender waist
and powerful legs, suggestive of strength beyond average. His
white campaign hat was thrust back on shortish dusty blond
hair. Tanned by the elements, the face it exposed was handsome without being eye-catching. Intelligent in its lines, its gray
eyes and a mouth which, though firm, could smile easily, indicated he was far from a rank-conscious bullying braggart holding his post merely as a result of family influence. Instead, he
had the indefinable air of a born leader who had matured early
and beyond his years in the harsh realities of war.

The small Texan's physique was enhanced by the uniform he
wore in a way that civilian attire would never achieve. However, despite being a disciplinarian of the finest kind—one who
lived by the spirit rather than the wording of military regulations—he was clearly not averse to breaking some of the Confederate States' stipulations with regard to dress and equipment. His tunic had the proscribed double row of buttons,
seven to the row, four inches wide at the top and two at the
bottom, but it lacked the skirt "extending halfway between hip
and knee." Like the cuffs of the sleeves and stripes down the
legs of his tight-fitting riding breeches, its "stand up" collar was
of the correct cavalry yellow. However, it was open, and instead of the official black cravat, his neck was encircled by a
flowing scarlet silk bandana. On his sleeves, rising from the
wrist to the bend of the elbow, was the elaborate double gold
thread Austrian-knot "chicken gut" insignia of his rank. As a
further indication that he was a captain—more easy to read
than the number of threads—there being no epaulettes, he had
three one-inch-long, half-inch-wide gold bars on his collar. He,
too, wore a *buscadero* pattern gunbelt, but his supported a
matched brace of bone-handled Army Colts in open-topped
cross-draw holsters.

Having been assigned to patrol in the direction of the bridge over the Mushogen River and see if it could be destroyed, Dusty had known he was faced with a formidable task. Never one to throw away the lives of his men recklessly, he had spent twenty-four hours in the vicinity studying the situation without the presence of himself and his company being discovered. However, the nature of the terrain had precluded any hope of launching a surprise attack by day. Nor, due to the full moon, would it be more feasible at night. Regardless of the latter, his very competent half-Kiowa scout had contrived to reconnoiter the camp at close quarters. Near enough, in fact, to overhear Buller instructing Packard to have the guard ready to march out early in the morning whether their relief—which had apparently not arrived before noon instead of shortly after dawn on three previous occasions—had put in an appearance or not. Ever ready to turn a situation to his advantage, the small Texan had outlined a plan which he considered would allow the assignment to be carried out with the minimum of casualties among his men.

With the exception of five men and a sergeant, who were to try to lure away the relief guard should it appear at the appointed time, Dusty had left the company under the command of his cousin, First Lieutenant Charles William Henry ("Red") Blaze. While the visibility would have been too great during the night hours for so large a body of men to make the approach undetected, he and Kiowa had contrived to reach the bushes closest to the bridge without being located by the lax sentries despite each of them carrying a small keg of gunpowder and fuse cord wrapped in waterproof tarpaulin.

Although the two Texans had been prepared to hide in the water beneath the overhanging foliage, the need had not arisen. The Yankees, instead of having taken the vital precaution of searching such a potentially dangerous area, had prepared to march off as soon as their commanding officer had risen. Then Red had brought Company C into view and everything started to happen as Dusty required.

With the attention of the Yankees devoted entirely to the

main body, the small Texan and his scout had set about their task. They were aware that, regardless of how well the distraction was succeeding, time might not be on their side. For one thing, the relief guard might not have taken the bait and could be on their way. Therefore they could not delay in commencing their preparations. Unfortunately, the only way they could reach the bridge was by leaving the concealment of the bushes and crossing open ground which would otherwise have been in plain view of its supposed defenders.

At first, it had seemed the plan was completely successful. However, as the two Texans were reaching the end of the bridge, they found that not all of the Yankees had become so engrossed in the pursuit as to have forgotten its existence.

"God damn it!" Kiowa said, watching Cogshill charging recklessly down the slope. "I just knowed he was going to be trouble from the start!"

"He's regular army and a damned sight smarter than the major," Dusty replied, having reached the conclusion from studying Buller and the lieutenant. Then he stiffened as the crackling of gunfire arose from beyond the rim. "We'd best hope Red and Billy Jack can keep the rest of them from coming back!"

"If they can't, or the relief guard's got here to cut them off," the sergeant answered, sharing his superior's realization that the shooting had commenced somewhat earlier than it was anticipated, "could be you 'n' me're in more 'n' just a mite of trouble, Cap'n Dusty!"

8

We'll Give Him Cogshill

"Goldarn and consarn it, I just *knowed* something'd go wrong, Mr. Blaze!" Sergeant Major Billy Jack asserted, with something like a complaining whine in his Texas drawl. "That Yankee luff's heading back!"

"Are any of them following him?" inquired the second in command of Company C of the Texas Light Cavalry, aware that the speaker had been carrying out the duty of watching what happened behind them.

"Not yet," Billy Jack admitted, sounding almost disappointed at being unable to reply in the affirmative.

Tall, gangling, the sergeant major had a long face which appeared to express sorrow and misery, but which in fact hid a humorous intelligence and what was claimed to be the best fund of dirty stories in the Confederate Army of Arkansas and North Texas. His *kepi* was tilted back at an apparently impossible angle on close-cropped black hair and his doleful features were tanned oak brown by exposure to the elements. Regardless of the prominent Adam's apple that emerged from the open neck of his cadet gray tunic, making him seem even more scrawny, he was as tough as whang leather and skilled in the use of the two Colt 1860 Army revolvers he carried.

"Reckon we'd best go back right now and make sure they don't get took with the notion," decided First Lieutenant Charles William Henry ("Red") Blaze, who duplicated the attire of his superior except that his holsters were positioned for a low cavalry twist draw and his Army Colts had walnut handles.

"Yo!" Billy Jack assented immediately, although he knew the company was not supposed to turn upon their pursuers until farther from the rim.

There were those who might have experienced grave doubts over the advisability of placing Red Blaze in a position of such responsibility, but the lanky sergeant major was not one of them. He was aware that, given such an assignment, the young lieutenant could be counted upon to discard an apparently reckless nature and behave with the competence of an efficient fighting leader.[1]

Urged on by Major Gerald Buller, who was in the lead only because he was much better mounted than the rest of them, Company A of the New Hampstead Volunteers were experiencing the exhilaration that arose from the sight of their fleeing enemies' backs. Waving his Tiffany-handled Navy Colt wildly, while exhorting his men to greater efforts, Buller was also thinking how he might word his report to discredit First Lieutenant Kirby Cogshill and keep all the acclaim for having protected the vitally important bridge over the Mushogen River for himself. Before he could draw any conclusions on the matter, other and less enjoyable issues were demanding his attention.

1. Further information regarding the sometimes contradictory character and exploits of First Lieutenant Charles William Henry "Red" Blaze can be found in various volumes of the *Civil War* and Floating Outfit series. J. T. E.

Suddenly and more swiftly than even Buller of the Yankees could believe was possible, the "cowardly Rebel scum" were no longer fleeing.

Obeying the command yelled by Red, although it was given sooner than expected, the Texans wheeled around their fast-running mounts with the skill acquired by what amounted to a lifetime in the saddle. Therefore, in a remarkably short time, they had changed from a "terrified flight" to charging at their erstwhile pursuers.

Alarmed by the drastic alteration in the behavior of their intended victims, those of the Volunteers who were not already doing so opened fire. As on their previous volley, they were still too far away. Even expert marksmen and horsemen could have achieved only a moderate result. Due to a disinclination among their superiors toward incurring the expense of providing the requisite powder and bullets, the enlisted men had only rarely been allowed to practice with the handguns which were their sole weapons. Nor were their mounts used to hearing the cracking of their weapons at such close quarters. Startled by the commotion, the horses reacted in a manner that rendered any hope of improving the aim even less likely.

In addition to riding well-trained animals and using ammunition looted from the Yankees, the Texans were given every opportunity to retain or improve skill with arms, and they were at no such disadvantage. What was more, while they, too, were volunteers, competent leadership and past experience had turned them into efficient veterans who had seen much combat. Ignoring the lead that occasionally whistled by, they were holding their fire until close enough for it to prove effective.

Just as startled by the unexpected developments as were his enlisted men, Buller nevertheless recollected advice he had frequently heard expounded by the regular army officers. According to them, the best way to dissuade an enemy force was to shoot down its leader. With that in mind, seeing the red-haired Rebel lieutenant—campaign hat now dangling by its chinstrap across broad shoulders—coming straight at him, he prepared to put the information to use by bringing up and aligning the ornate revolver.

Unfortunately for the major, Red was equally aware of the advice. He acted upon it with skill and precision. Having secured the split-end reins around the low horn of his double-girthed Texas range saddle, which offered a firmer seat than Buller's eastern rig, he had an Army Colt in each hand. Controlling the well-trained horse by pressure from his knees, he opened fire an instant before his would-be assailant could commence.

Left, right, left, right, the weapons thundered.

The speed at which Red was moving caused the white smoke of the detonated powder to be whipped away, allowing him to see what he was doing. Controlling and thumb-cocking the Colts on their recoil, he contrived to change their respective point of aim slightly between each discharge. As the fourth .44-caliber round lead ball was sent upon its way, its predecessor ploughed into the chest of the Yankee major. An instant later, while Buller was reeling under the impact, the following lead punctured a blue-rimmed hole in the center of his forehead. Sliding from the saddle, he crashed lifeless to the ground.

The position in which the inexperienced Volunteers found themselves was one capable of demoralizing far better trained and disciplined soldiers. Even those who had not yet emptied their revolvers were finding it increasingly difficult to control their mounts. To add further to their consternation, although none of their bullets were taking effect, men about them were being shot by their clearly far more competent attackers.

Such a desperate predicament might have been alleviated, perhaps even overcome, by capable leadership. Unfortunately for the Volunteers, they were deprived of this. The one best suited to at least attempt to extricate them, Cogshill, was already dashing back in the hope of saving the bridge. While—by virtue of his rank—Buller was the logical candidate, it was unlikely he had the ability to effect anything even if he had not fallen victim to the accurate shooting of the Texas-born lieutenant.

Nor was Sergeant Major Alden Packard available to try and rally the enlisted men. Struck in the head by a wild bullet from one of the Volunteers, his horse collapsed beneath him as his superior was going down. Throwing himself clear and losing his Manhattan Navy revolver, he concluded discretion to be the better part of valor. Allowing himself to sprawl face down on the ground, ignoring the pounding of hooves all around him, he lay giving an impersonation of a corpse and allowed the remnants of Company A to try to extract themselves from the dire straits into which they had been led by their incompetent commanding officer.

Demoralized and left leaderless, the surviving Volunteers began to discard their revolvers. Leaving behind those who were unhorsed, wounded, or dead, the former taking flight on foot, they scattered like quail being flushed from a meadow, and the fear of death was encouraging each to goad his horse to greater efforts.

"Bugler!" Red bellowed, reining his mount to a halt and watching their enemies scattering. "Sound 'Cease Fire' and 'Recall'!"

"How's about their arms and wounded, Mr. Blaze?" Billy Jack inquired, as the enlisted men of Company C called off their pursuit of the fleeing Volunteers in response to the calls from the bugle.

"What I saw, they were mostly toting Joslyns and Pettingills, but some had what looked like Navy Colts," Red answered, glancing around, having drawn an erroneous conclusion from noticing the Manhattans and Metropolitans, which bore a deliberate resemblance to the far superior revolvers he had named last. Then, seeing a man of his company approaching from the south leading two horses, he went on, "Way Sandy's coming in, I'd say the relief guard's on its way. We'll leave their wounded for them to tend and go let Cousin Dusty know what's doing."

Although the lanky sergeant major accepted his superior was making real good sense, neither realized they were helping to pave the way for their commanding officer to face one of the most serious and soul-searching decisions of his young life.

"Damn it to hell!" shouted Captain Dustine Edward Marsden ("Dusty") Fog, watching the blue-clad young lieutenant closing rapidly and drawing the revolver from his holster. "Why couldn't it have been that loud-mouthed major who came back?"

Uttering the comment, the small Texan allowed the bundle wrapped in tarpaulin to slip from his grasp. Flashing across almost too fast for the human eye to follow, his right hand enfolded the butt of the near-side Army Colt. Sweeping it from its carefully designed holster, forefinger staying outside the triggerguard, and thumb refraining from coiling around the spur of the hammer until *after* the seven-and-a-half-inches-long "civilian"-pattern barrel was turning away from him,[2] he made ready to fire.[3] Not, however, at waist level and by instinctive alignment. Although it was being closed fast, the distance to his intended mark was too great for such a method to offer the kind of accuracy he required. As the left hand rose to join the right on the butt with the facility offered by his completely ambidextrous prowess, a natural trait enhanced by constant practice all through his life—perhaps to help distract from his lack of height in a land of tall men—he elevated the weapon until able to take sight along the barrel. Regardless of having taken this precaution, he squeezed off a shot in just over a second after the movement was commenced.

Swiftly though the Army Colt had been drawn and fired, the result was indicative of the skill which would in the not too distant future gain the small Texan acclaim as the Rio Hondo gun wizard. Flying almost precisely as it was intended, the lead struck Cogshill in the right shoulder. For all that, the lieutenant might have counted himself fortunate. Instead of using a soft ball, which tended to "mushroom" badly on impact, Dusty

2. When intended to fulfil military contracts, Colt 1860 Army Model revolvers had barrels eight inches in length. J. T. E.
3. An example of just how dangerous failure to take such precautions could prove is given in: *The Fast Gun.* J. T. E.

had loaded the revolvers with shaped bullets. What was more, so carefully was it dispatched, the missile missed the bones in the area and passed through, inflicting a less serious injury than would otherwise have been the case.

Pain and shock knifed through the young lieutenant. Combining with an involuntary swerve by his horse, alarmed at having a weapon discharged so close ahead, it caused him to be toppled from his saddle. As he was going down, he lost his grip on his revolver. However, on landing, he forced himself to disregard the agony he was suffering and rolled toward the weapon. Managing to snatch it up with his left hand, he began to force himself into a kneeling position. As he was doing so, he saw the Indian-dark Rebel sergeant had dropped a tarpaulin-wrapped bundle and was already darting toward him. Gritting his teeth, he prepared to try and sell his life dearly.

"Don't kill him, Kiowa!" Dusty shouted, watching his companion swinging free the Henry rifle.

Giving no indication of whether or not he had heard the command, the sergeant reached his objective. However, even without the order he had received, he had no desire to take the life of a young man as courageous as the "Yankee luff" had proved to be. Furthermore, he was aware that his superior had not shot to kill. This implied Captain Fog wanted the lieutenant left alive for some reason. Therefore, while he had liberated the rifle, he only intended to use it as a firearm as a last resource. Concluding such measures were not called for, he employed it as a club. Swinging the barrel against the side of the head, but with less than the full force of which he was capable, he rendered Cogshill unconscious before the retrieved Army Colt could start to threaten his or his superior's life.

"Didn't never have no notion to make wolf bait of him, Cap'n Dusty," Kiowa claimed, turning toward the small Texan. "I float my stick 'long of you on it, he's too brave to gun down for keeps."

"He was brave enough and smart to boot," Dusty agreed, returning his revolver to its holster. "Leather his Colt for him, then we'll get the bridge set ready for blowing. Sounds like

Cousin Red had to turn and fight sooner than we counted on. Him and the boys might be needing to get across the river real fast, that happening."

Raising his head cautiously, Sergeant Major Packard lowered it again almost immediately. Although the Texans who had decimated and scattered his company were already riding down the slope, another half dozen were approaching at a gallop. Waiting until they had gone by, he made sure no more of them were in the vicinity. Only when satisfied he could do so in safety did he come to his feet. Looking around, he discovered that he had not been alone in playing possum. A short distance away, having kept a similarly surreptitious observation, a burly and equally brutal-looking corporal was also rising, displaying the same absence of having suffered any kind of injury.

"What happened to you, Silky?" Packard asked, paying no attention to the half a dozen genuinely wounded enlisted men who were lying and trying to rise from where they had fallen.

"Hoss throwed me," Corporal John Silkin replied truthfully, but without going on to explain that he, too, had considered it would be safer to play dead. "Those lousy Reb sons of bitches sure suckered us good, Pack!"

"Yeah," the sergeant major agreed, accepting the employment of his nickname from a man who had acted as bruiser and bully under his command in the service of the Buller family. "They did at that!"

Having supported the corporal's point of view, Packard still showed no indication of offering aid to the wounded. Instead, followed by Silkin, he went to where their commanding officer lay facedown on the ground. One glance at the gory mess which was the back of Buller's head told him nothing could be done by way of first aid.

"He's cashed in," the sergeant major announced unnecessarily, then collected the ornately butted Navy Colt from where it had fallen after leaving the dead hand of its owner. "Wouldn't you know he'd have a good gun like this while we've been given any goddamned cheap trash they could get even cheaper."

"Sure would," Silkin replied, ever the sycophant. He had turned over and searched Buller's pockets, extracting a thick wallet from inside the tunic. "Reckon he won't be needing this where he's going, Pack."

"They do say paper money burns, Silky," the sergeant major answered, "so we'll split it down the middle, but put the wallet back in his kick."

"How the hell're we going to get back to camp?" Silkin wanted to know, after the division of the money was made and the wallet returned.

"Easy enough," Packard claimed and pointed. "Company E's headed this way, late like always."

At that moment, two explosions rang out so close together they merged into a single sound. Spinning around, the pair of hardcases ran toward the rim. Halting on top, they stared into the valley. It was apparent even to Silkin, who was more muscular and brutal than intelligent, that their company had failed in the duty to which they had been assigned. Furthermore, despite Company E approaching fast, the men who had brought about the failure were safe from pursuit and attempts to take revenge.

Already the Rebels were on the northern bank of the Mushogen River, but the Volunteers would have great difficulty in going after them. They had ridden across the bridge and such a convenient means of reaching the other side was no longer available. Shattered by the explosive charges, much of it was already floating downstream. While it would be possible to swim across with horses, provided the riders had the requisite skill, the men responsible for the destruction were waiting on the opposite rim to counter any such attempt.

"Holy Mother!" Silkin said. "They've sure busted up that son of a bitch. It's lucky for us's Moe Buller's gone to Washington."

"It'd be easier was he here," Packard corrected him, having greater perception than his companion and being better able to appreciate the full ramifications of the situation, although his interest was less directed at the strategic implications than upon how he personally might be affected by the demolition of the bridge.

"How come?" the corporal inquired, coarse features expressing his puzzlement. "What I know of Moe, he's going to be riled as all hell over what's happened."

"And so's that bastard from the Third Cavalry's running things in his place while he's away," the sergeant major pointed out.

"Yeah!" Silkin grunted, nodding vehemently. Then he continued with something close to petulance in his harsh voice, "I can't see why Moe didn't leave Fatso Meacher to run things for him."

"It'd been easier if he had," Packard confessed pensively, but did not offer to explain that Colonel Michael ("Fatso") Meacher of their regiment was junior in length of service and time of appointment to Colonel Iain McDonald, commanding officer of the regular Third Cavalry.

Instead of taking time to instruct the corporal in the matter of military seniority, from which not even a regiment of volunteers favored by the area's commanding general was immune, the sergeant major gave all his attention to the future. Having been associated with the Buller family for several years, he had come to know them very well and felt certain the elder brother would do everything possible to prevent blame for the destruction of the bridge from falling where it belonged, on his brother. However, such a sentiment would not be caused by feelings of love, or even fondness, for his sibling.

A man consumed by ambition, Moses J. Buller was ruthless in his determination to have his desires fulfilled. Experience had taught him that, as a result of their family ties, the misdeeds of Gerald could have an adverse effect upon him even if he was unaware they had taken place. Therefore, in the past, he had on more than one occasion been compelled to take drastic steps to keep his much less intelligent younger brother from the consequences of various far from harmless escapades and sometimes more than minor infractions of the law.

Unless Packard was badly mistaken, a situation demanding

such protective action had once more occurred. Nor would the need for it be removed by the death of the younger Buller. Due to his crass stupidity, as the sergeant major now knew the pursuit of the Rebels to have been, his superior had cost the Union Army of Arkansas a much needed, even vital, bridge. What was more, it emphasized that the brigadier general was no more able than his predecessor to cope with the enemy. He would be furious when learning that such a fiasco had taken place, particularly as the responsibility for it could be laid upon his sibling. Offered the means by which some of the blame could be placed elsewhere, perhaps all of it, he would be grateful to the man who made this possible.

Watching Cogshill struggling erect by the ruined bridge, a savage grin came to the far from prepossessing face of the burly sergeant major. Remembering the thinly veiled hostility between the volunteer and regular officers of the regiment, added to the knowledge he had acquired on certain military matters, he concluded this could be turned to his advantage.

"How'd you mean, 'easier,' Pack?" Silkin asked, breaking into his superior's train of thought.

"Moe's not going to take it kind that the bridge's been blowed up, 'specially with his brother running things when it happened," the sergeant major explained. "And, knowing him like I do, he'll be looking for somebody else to take the blame. So we'll give him Cogshill."

"Cogshill?" repeated the corporal, face blank with incomprehension.

"Nobody else but," Packard affirmed. "He's the goddamned bow-necked regular officer's knows all about such, so he should've warned Gerry boy what the Rebs was up to. Instead, he stopped down where it was safe and let us get led into a trap." Glancing to where the relief guard was almost within hearing distance, he finished, "Leave *me* do the talking and back up everything I say. Handled right, Silky, there's *money* in this for you and me."

9

I'll Get Rid of Lincoln

"Good *afternoon*, General!" Mary Wilkinson greeted, glancing sourly around the sitting room into which she had been fetched by Second Lieutenant Robert Cryer, after having waited downstairs for over an hour. Her all too obvious displeasure had been created by two sources of annoyance. Since her arrival at the hotel, finding herself unable to conceal some of the injuries given to her face by the fight, she had been subjected to much unwelcome attention and, among those familiar with her background, what she had known to be mocking commiseration over her appearance. Nor had her mood been mellowed by having discovered the identity of one person responsible for the delay. "I'm so *pleased* you can spare the time to see *me* at last!"

"I said I'd see you," Brigadier General Moses J. Buller replied, but the words were not delivered in anything approaching an apology. "And I sent for you to come up as soon as I could."

"I was told you were occupied," the yellowish-brunette admitted, swinging her gaze from the table, which was littered with the debris of a single person's meal, to the door of the main bedroom. Then she returned her gaze to the man she had come to visit. "Is that goddamned redhead still with you?"

"No!" the general growled, glaring at his visitor through bloodshot eyes, in a way that warned her the subject was one he would not tolerate being continued. "She's *not* still with me!"

There was good cause for Buller to be in a bad humor where "Françoise" was concerned.

Waking up that morning, suffering from what he still assumed to have been nothing more than the aftereffects of excessive drinking, the general had felt far too ill to care that he found himself alone in the bedroom. What was more, he soon had other things on his mind. Hearing him vomiting into the chamberpot, Cryer had entered followed by Captain Raymond Berry from the office of the provost marshal. Although they had come to tell him that First Lieutenant Martin Flannery had been found dead in mysterious and still unexplained circumstances, the condition in which he had been left by the drugged brandy rendered him almost incapable of comprehending anything he was being told. However, succor had been forthcoming from an unexpected source. Having arrived with a letter from George Wigg, Thaddeus Barnes had offered his assistance on being informed by the surviving *aide-de-camp* of the general's "indisposition." The concoction produced by the butler, apparently from ingredients obtained in the kitchen of the hotel, had proved sufficiently efficacious to allow its recipient to understand what had happened.

When the captain had started to ask questions, it had become apparent that he was not aware of the existence of the "redhead." This had come about as a result of Cryer having appreciated the need for discretion when, on being aroused by Berry in the early hours of the morning, they had gone into the main bedroom to tell Buller about Flannery. Finding they were unable to wake their superior and realizing that the girl was missing, the lieutenant had concluded she must have left in disgust when her "customer" had succumbed to the drunken stupor.

Knowing Buller and—due to the reticence of Flannery—having had no reason to suspect that "Françoise" was in any way connected with the killing, Cryer had considered it would be impolitic to mention her. The general had the kind of mentality that would resent its becoming known he had been associating with a prostitute, particularly as she appeared to have deserted him in such unflattering circumstances.

On being told of the presence and subsequent disappearance of the "redhead," previous experience had made it unnecessary for Berry to ask why nothing was said about her during his earlier visit. Being aware of the need for discretion where such matters were concerned, the captain had waited to see how the general reacted to hearing of the omission and, when it was passed over without criticism, followed the lead he was given by accepting she did not appear to have anything to do with the killing.

However, despite an examination having established that none of Buller's property was missing, he had stated his intention of visiting the brothel personally and questioning "Françoise." Although his real reason was to persuade her to accompany him to Arkansas as had been arranged, before he could set off, Mrs. Amy Cutler had arrived and demanded rather than requested an interview with him. On being admitted, she had said that Miss Wilkinson was downstairs at the desk. Sending Cryer to deal with the brunette, the general had asked the madam why she wished to see him and if she wanted to speak in private. She had replied that she was aware of Berry's official status and assumed the same business had brought them both to the hotel.

According to the story told by the madam, the "redhead" had returned to the brothel in the early hours of the morning and taken almost immediate departure without reporting to her. Instead, while collecting her belongings from the room assigned to her, "Françoise" had explained to the other "young lady" who shared the room what had taken place to cause her flight from the hotel. While going in search of a lavatory after the general had "fallen asleep" (realizing he might have need of the chamberpot beneath the bed on "waking up"), she had been molested by Flannery. In the ensuing struggle, a push had caused him to fall through the window. Being aware that he came from a very wealthy and influential family, who she had felt sure would be determined to prevent the truth becoming known, she had stated her intention of taking up an offer of sponsorship for her ability at fighting received from a person who she believed was sufficiently important to be able to guarantee her safety.

Acting in the manner of a brothel keeper genuinely enraged by having been deprived of a lucrative employee, Mrs. Cutler had demanded to be told whether Buller was, or knew the identity of, the sponsor. Declaring he was not, but refraining from mentioning he had had designs along those lines, he confessed that the "redhead" had spoken of such a person without supplying any name. Asked by Berry if she could suggest the identity of the sponsor, the madam had admitted that she could think of four possibilities. She had also asserted that she would supply the names of the quartet, but only if he and the general signed a statement saying this was done at their insistence and absolving her of all responsibility should there be objections from any of the four to being questioned on the matter. The impression she had conveyed was that each of the quartet was sufficiently prominent and influential for there to be most unpleasant consequences if any hint of their bizarre taste in entertainment should become known outside the immediate circle of fellow devotees. Satisfied she had achieved her purpose in that direction, she had next pointed out how the well-connected family of the dead lieutenant would not be enamored of the reason for his death being treated in anything other than a confidential fashion, and this might prove impossible if the search for "Françoise" was continued.

It said much for Mrs. Cutler's reputation as a confidante to many of the most important men in the hierarchy of Washington that the general and the captain had accepted the line of thought she had created without raising either questions or objections. In fact, knowing with whom she was dealing in each case, she had felt sure this would happen. Furthermore, in tribute to her shrewd judgment of character, the affair turned out even more satisfactorily than she had anticipated.

Although he was far from distressed at having lost a subordinate who was never respectful or—he suspected—entirely trustworthy, Buller wanted to avoid any chance of antagonizing the Flannery family. With that in mind, he had proposed a solution. It could be claimed the lieutenant had been killed in a gallant and, as no thefts were reported, successful attempt to drive off a gang of thieves surprised in the passage outside the suite. This would, he had declared, be far more acceptable to the family than having the sordid truth made known.

Being a professional "office filler," and therefore concerned that he should remain in the comfortable sinecure which kept him clear of the more dangerous aspects of soldiering, and knowing that pursuing a line of inquiry about Flannery's death would be likely to put his position in jeopardy, Berry had been only too willing to concur. He had claimed that, as there had been a spate of such robberies in the city, he would make his report in the manner proposed by the general. Knowing the kind of man he was, and aware that such robberies were indeed taking place, the madam had felt sure he would comply and had meant to offer a similar "explanation" for the killing if Buller had not done so.

With the meeting concluded to the satisfaction of himself and Mrs. Cutler, although he was unaware of the reason for the latter's satisfaction, Buller had not sent for Mary when his two visitors had taken their departure. In response to a hint from the madam, he had decided to delay seeing her until he was more presentable. Despite the soldier who acted as his servant having failed to report for duty, his task was made unexpectedly easy. Having waited in the main bedroom to take any answer there might be to the letter from his employer, Barnes had offered his services. Claiming he was never one to waste time, he had taken the liberty of "tidying up" and would, if the general wished, perform the duties neglected by the absent servant.

Already impressed by the stimulant prepared by the butler, Buller had agreed. He had soon discovered Barnes to be far superior in every way to the missing man. Using the voice pipe installed in the bedroom which led to the kitchen, the butler had ordered a breakfast acceptable to a still somewhat queasy stomach. Then he had set about washing and shaving Buller and combing his hair. With that done, apologizing for not having had the time to clean it adequately, he had produced another uniform and pair of boots with an unaccustomed shine. While eating the food, the general had read the letter from Wigg asking if they could meet again in the future. Deducing this implied there was no urgency and certain the undertaker could do nothing to further his own plans, he had asked whether Barnes was contented. Admitting he found the parsimonious nature of his present employer distasteful, the butler had accepted the offer to accompany Buller to Arkansas. Feeling in a more amiable mood as a result of the ministrations he had received, he had announced he was ready to meet his next visitor and she was summoned.

"Anyways," the general continued after a moment, deciding there was nothing to be gained by antagonizing the brunette—in fact, as she might be an acceptable substitute for the departed "Françoise," he could be the loser if he did so—"I don't reckon you came here to meet *her*."

"I didn't," Mary admitted truthfully, being more relieved than disappointed by the absence of the "redhead," her comment of the previous evening notwithstanding. "I came because you said you would tell me about whatever it is Aaranovitch is doing for you. I hope it's worthwhile?"

"Worthwhile?" Buller repeated. "You can bet your life it's *worthwhile* and more!"

"Will it take long for you to tell me?" the brunette inquired with thinly veiled sarcasm, glancing pointedly at a chair by the table.

"You better sit down," the general ordered rather than offered, showing not the slightest embarrassment over the need for the reminder. As Mary and Cryer did so, he went on, "By god, yes. You've never been more right than when you asked if it was *worthwhile*. It's going to win the war for me!"

"It sounds as if the son of a bitch will do all you say," Mary declared, at the conclusion of a description of the experiment Buller had witnessed the previous night. "But there's one thing stopping you."

"What'd that be?" the general challenged.

"Lincoln!" the brunette replied.

"Lincoln?" Buller queried, despite a suspicion that he could supply the answer.

"Lincoln," Mary repeated. "Hell, General, you know that mealymouthed Sucker State jury-fixer is too softhearted to let you use stuff like that against the Rebs!"

"It'll have been used against them before he hears about it," Buller claimed. "Nobody apart from Aaranovitch and Montreigen have seen what it does, or even know about it."

"That girl you took with you knows!" Cryer put in, not without a suggestion of malicious satisfaction.

"Did she see what you saw?" Mary demanded.

"Yes!" Buller admitted, and his surly face showed apprehension.

"Where is she?" the brunette snapped.

"She ran out on me last night," the general answered and explained the circumstances as he had been led to believe they had taken place, concluding, "But she wouldn't say anything about what she saw."

"How do you know?" Mary challenged, seeing a chance to obtain revenge upon the girl who had beaten her. "If it was me, I would make sure she *couldn't* talk about it."

"I don't know who she went to," Buller pointed out.

"Cutler does," the brunette asserted.

"That's likely," the general conceded. "She admitted she knew four men who might be willing to take Frenchie on to fight for them, and I'm willing to bet she could take it closer than that."

"Then we'll have to make her 'take it closer'!" Mary stated viciously. "And I'll see to it she does!"

"Like hell you will!" the general refused vehemently. "Or, if you're aiming to do anything to her, don't let *me* hear of it. She's in with too many real important people around this town for anything like that."

"Then what do you intend to do?" the brunette inquired, having received an almost identical response to her proposal of reprisals against Mrs. Cutler from the two men she had had brought to see her the previous night.

"I'm thinking on it," Buller replied evasively. "Weren't you saying something about having a couple of fellers who'd do things for you at Wigg's last night?"

"I was," Mary conceded, then glanced at the lieutenant before continuing, "When did you say you're leaving for Arkansas, General?"

"I told Montreigen to be ready to pull out just after noon today," Buller replied, taking what he realized had been a hint from the brunette. "Go and tell him he can get moving, Mr. Cryer. If she's so minded, Miss Wilkinson can come with me when I follow in the coach."

"I'm not packed ready for leaving," the *aide-de-camp* objected, realizing something was in the air and wanting to be party to whatever it might be.

"You'll have plenty of time to do it when you get back," Buller answered, scowling angrily. "But I want everything on its way today, well before nightfall, or I'll make somebody wish it had been!"

"Yes, sir!" Cryer assented, but with bad grace.

"Well," Buller said, after the lieutenant had taken a reluctant departure from the suite. "What were you going to say last night?"

"What the dinner should have been all about if that yellow-bellied son of a bitch, Horace Trumpeter, hadn't started the others backing off from it," Mary replied, interspersing her words with needless profanities. "Killing that old bastard, Lincoln. And, as far as you're concerned, it's even more urgent to have that done now. If he gets just one hint of what you're going to use against those Rebel sons of bitches in Arkansas, he'll have you stopped."

"Go on!" Buller prompted, as the brunette allowed her tirade to trail to an end in a way that implied there was much more to be said.

"I'll get rid of Lincoln for you," Mary promised.

"You?" the general challenged.

"Not *me* personally," the brunette admitted. "But those two men I mentioned will do it, if they think the price is high enough."

"I don't reckon you had them with you last night," Buller stated rather than asked, thinking disdainfully of the trio who had accompanied Mary to the dinner party.

"No, although they have their uses," the brunette replied, more as a defense of her judgment in choosing associates than out of any sense of loyalty to her three young adherents. "They're a couple of copperheads who deserted rather than chance being caught by the Rebs. But each is a dead shot and I've got them a Sharps rifle apiece, which will kill at over a mile. There's a place well inside that distance that offers a clear shot at the study window where Lincoln stands looking out regularly. Either one could hit him from there, and with both trying, it makes things doubly certain."

"You're sure they'll do it?"

"They'll kill their own mothers, was the pay enough and they believed they could get away with doing it."

"That kind don't strike me's being any too reliable in a pinch," Buller stated dubiously.

"Nor would they be," Mary conceded. "So I intend to make sure they aren't able to be *unreliable* as soon as they've done their job. But even then they'll still be of use to you and me."

"How do you mean?" the general queried, genuinely puzzled.

"They'll be killed as soon as they've shot him," the brunette explained, as calmly as if she were discussing the weather. "And there's going to be enough information on them to 'prove' they aren't copperheads, but genuine Rebs who came here to kill Lincoln. With him dead, there's going to be so much confusion getting somebody to take his place, nobody will give a damn what happens out in Arkansas. Then, when word comes back of how you've licked those peckerwood bastards, Lincoln being so popular, everybody will be clamoring for enough of that liquid of yours to finish off the rest of them."

"You've thought this all out pretty well," Buller praised, then his brows narrowed in suspicion. "Or did you *know* what Aaranovitch was up to?"

"Not until you told me about it," Mary replied reassuringly. "I'd got the rest of it figured out, though. Your liquid just makes his death that much better for us."

"Who's going to kill those fellers?" the general inquired. "I wouldn't want to leave it to the three you had with you last night."

"Or me," Mary seconded. "Can you let me have somebody?"

"The only one I'd want to count on is Montreigen," Buller stated, then he growled an imprecation and went on, "but I've sent him off with Aaranovitch!"

"So much the better," Mary claimed. "It will give him a perfect alibi. When you catch up, have him come back in civilian clothes and meet me. We'll do it together and follow on horseback to join you along the way."

Looking at the shapely brunette, the general concluded he had sold her short the previous evening. Instead of being no more than a loudmouthed young woman trying to act like a man, she was shrewd and had the completely ruthless nature required to pull off her daring plan. There was, to his warped way of thinking, something else in favor of letting her join his entourage. She might make an adequate substitute for the departed "Françoise." As she had proved at the dinner party, she was willing to fight and, perhaps, was subject to a similar sexual stimulation after being engaged in physical combat. While she had lost at Wigg's mansion, she had performed better than any other woman he had seen with the exception of the "redhead." What was more, as he had envisaged for the "French Canadian" girl, she would be the unexpected combatant offering a source of lucrative wagering.

"All right!" Buller said enthusiastically. "We'll play it the way you want!"

"I thought you might," Mary asserted. "Where is that red-haired bitch?"

"I don't know," Buller replied. "She ran out on me last night after I fell asleep."

"It's lucky for her she did!" the brunette declared. "I just hope I meet her again sometime when she doesn't have that fat blond whore to help her. Shall we get going, General?"

"Sure," Buller replied. "I'll tell Barnes to get my things together."

"Barnes?" Mary repeated, noticing how the general glanced toward the door of the main bedroom.

"Wigg's butler," Buller explained. "Or rather he was Wigg's butler. I've hired him this morning."

"He's in *there*?" the brunette demanded, looking at the door.

"Sure," the General agreed. "But don't worry, he's busy working and couldn't have heard what we've been saying."

If Buller had been able to see into the main bedroom, he would have learned he was in error.

Standing by the connecting door, Barnes held the top of a glass against the panel, and its base was pressed to his left ear. This simple device had allowed him to overhear the entire conversation.

10

You Want Us to Down
Old Honest Abe

"Well, now, fancy miss," David Blunkett remarked, his voice indicating his origins were south of the Mason-Dixon line, darting a glance at William Kendall. "That's a right tidy sum you're offering Cousin Billy 'n' me. Who-all's putting it up?"

"You're getting it," Mary Wilkinson replied. "Isn't that enough?"

Having traveled on horseback to the small farmhouse some seven miles north of Washington, the yellowish-brunette was dressed much as she had been when attending the dinner party at George Wigg's mansion, apart from having left off the cravat and cutaway jacket. However, suspended on the slings of a weapon belt about her slender waist, she was armed with an *épée de combat,* in the use of which she had considerable skill. She had already made sure the men she was visiting knew that. She had removed her cloak and hat on entering, leaving them on the chair by the door of the sitting room in which the meet-

ing was taking place shortly before ten o'clock on the day of
her interview with Brigadier General Moses J. Buller.

Tallish, lanky, with unprepossessing and unshaven faces, the
deserters wore the clothing suggestive of ordinary farmhands.
When appearing outside, giving an impression of working the
property, which belonged to one of Mary's uncles who was
serving with the army in the South, Blunkett walked with a
pronounced limp and Kendall carried his right arm in a leather
tube and sling to explain why two men of their age were not
serving in one of the fighting services.

"You can't get no more, can you?" Kendall asked, his accent
similar to that of his slightly taller cousin.

"No!" the brunette stated, although the sum she had been
authorized to pay by Buller was in excess of the amount quoted
when telling the deserters what was wanted from them. "But I
do have something to boot, I think you call it, which is worth
far more than just money."

"Ain't many things's I'd say is worth more'n *money!*"
Kendall growled. "Jewels, maybe, 'cepting a couple of poor old
country boys like us'd likely have a slew of trouble saying how
we come by 'em."

"It isn't *jewels*," Mary admitted.

"What'd it be then, fancy miss?" Blunkett inquired.

"Two *genuine* certificates of discharge from the army on the
grounds of ill health," the brunette explained. "With them and
the money, you can go anywhere you want throughout the
country without running the risk of being suspected as deserters."

"Hell!" Kendall snorted. "We're doing pretty well at that
right now, so I'd say my say for more money was I give my
druthers."

"How about *you,* Mr. Blunkett?" Mary said, knowing him to
be the more intelligent of the pair. "Do you want to spend the
rest of the war, at least, hiding out here and having to remem-
ber all the time you're supposed to have a crippled leg?"

"Well, no, ma'am, I can't rightly say's I do," said the taller
cousin. "Them certificates'd sure come in handy, us not taking

overkind to being tied to this old farm and hankering for some good times in a city. You wouldn't have 'em 'long of you, I reckon?"

"I *wouldn't*!" the brunette declared and nodded to where, looking nervous despite having a Colt 1860 Army revolver thrust prominently into his waistband, Eric Lubbock was standing by the door. "Nor has my friend. You'll get them and the money as soon as I see Lincoln go down and not a moment before."

"Don't you *trust* us?" Kendall growled.

"Not enough to give you everything you need to leave *before* you've earned it," Mary admitted frankly, but it was clear her next words were directed at the other deserter. "Now you can't blame me for *that,* can you?"

"I wouldn't've blamed you for being careful even had we been inter-duced all proper-like," Blunkett asserted amiably. "By grab, though, you surely put one over on us that night!"

Having deserted, after a narrow escape from capture by Confederate troops, who had an understandable antipathy toward Southrons serving in the Union Army and who were inclined to take lethally painful reprisals against any falling into their hands, the cousins had kept going until chance had led them to Washington. It had not been the intention of the pair to remain in the vicinity of the capital, but the matter was taken from their hands. Needing money, they had waylaid Mary and Alister Graham one night in the city's low-rent district. The young man had surrendered and pleaded not to be hurt, while offering his wallet, but she had proved a different proposition.

Diverting the attention of the pair by opening the front of her shirt and displaying her otherwise naked bosom, the brunette had produced a Smith & Wesson Army Model No. 2 revolver from the pocket of her cutaway coat. While its octagonal barrel had been reduced from six inches to two for ease of concealment and its caliber was only .32, its cylinder held five metallic case cartridges. What was more, not only had she withdrawn to a distance greater than they could hope to reach by using the clubs which were their only weapons, the facility she displayed in handling it warned she was far from making a gesture of harmless or panic-stricken defiance.

Always the quicker-witted of the cousins, realizing the futility of resistance, Blunkett had ordered Kendall to stand still. Then he had sought to avoid being turned over to the authorities by claiming they were a couple of sharpshooters on furlough and were trying to obtain money to rejoin their regiment after having been robbed of their uniform in a cheap brothel. When Graham had offered to fetch the police, Mary, ever ready to exploit any situation chance put her way, had told him to wait. Having drawn an accurate conclusion about their loyalties from their accents, she stated she did not believe the story. She had declared she would help the men provided they could prove to her satisfaction they were qualified as "snipers," although she used the current military description for that term. Accepting there was no other course open to them, unless they wished to chance either being shot or having local peace officers attracted to the vicinity, Blunkett had asserted that proof would be forthcoming if they were given a chance to show their skills.

Mary had been able to provide that chance. Having been asked to take care of the farm in the absence of her uncle, she had not kept on its hired hands, and she used it solely as a location at which she could practice her riding, shooting, and fencing. She had also found it allowed her to let her three companions fire the Sharps Model of 1852 breech loading percussion rifles she had obtained for a sinister purpose. They were .52 in caliber, equipped with a telescopic sight, and were the longest-ranged and most accurate shoulder arms available. However, she had very soon concluded none of the trio would ever become a sufficiently skilled marksman to do what she required.

Escorting the deserters to the property, in such a way that they had been given no opportunity of escaping, the brunette had satisfied herself that each possessed the ability to be regarded as a sharpshooter. Offering them a safe haven, with plenty of good food and liquor provided, she had then sought

financial and influential backing to put her scheme into operation. She had learned of the incautious way President Abraham
Lincoln frequently stood before the undraped window of his
study, and she had selected a place of concealment within the
range of the Sharps. While certain the pair could produce the
required result, she had known they would demand a much
larger sum of money and would also try to find out if somebody
of far greater importance than herself would be prepared to pay
more. She had attended the dinner party in the hope of gathering that information for herself. Despite the defeat she had
suffered threatening to put her scheme in jeopardy, it seemed
another turn of fate had provided her with the wealthy backer
she needed.

Although Major Saul Montreigen had not yet returned from
escorting David Aaranovitch, Mary had been too impatient to
wait for him. Instead, wanting to impress Buller with her efficiency, she had come to the farm to conclude the business arrangements with the deserters. Being disinclined to trust them
any further than was necessary, she had brought her three adherents, and all were armed. Knowing her limitations in its use,
she had left the Colt Model of 1851 Navy revolver—which she
owned in addition to the Smith & Wesson now in the pocket of
her cloak—in the holster attached to her horse's saddle. She
was placing her reliance upon the *épée,* as she could produce
and wield it with far greater speed.

The negotiations had not been protracted. On learning whom
they were required to kill, despite having served against their
home state, apparently giving their support to the Union, the
deserters had asked only how much they would be paid and
how they could escape when the task was completed. After
having accepted the price and agreed on the arrangements,
Blunkett had raised the point Mary had expected, yet had
hoped to avoid. It appeared at first to have passed notice, partly
due to the greed displayed by Kendall. However, her hope that
the subject was forgotten failed to materialize.

"Just who-all do you have behind you, fancy miss?" the

taller deserter went on, after the last remark about the way in which he and his cousin had met the brunette.

"What makes you think there is somebody?" Mary challenged.

"Well, now," Blunkett replied, "what we've heard when we snuck into town, you and your family ain't what I'd call real important folks. Not anywheres close enough to keep us safe should things go wrong."

"Who is?" the brunette inquired grimly, wondering when the pair had visited Washington in defiance of her orders to remain on the farm. "If anything should go wrong, which isn't likely as long as you do everything I tell you, *nobody* could be important enough to keep you safe."

"I don't mean's how we could be got out of it like all we'd done was get caught stealing chickens, fancy miss," the taller deserter corrected. "But a feller with enough pull, knowing's how we could put his neck in a noose 'long of our'n, would sure throw his weight to the harness should things go wrong regardless of you saying's how they can't. So, happen you want us to down old Honest Abe for you, we'll have to know who-all's back of you."

"That's fair enough," Mary conceded, deciding Blunkett was shrewder than she had anticipated and wondering whether he would consider Buller of sufficient importance or if she should name somebody of greater social prominence. Concluding it was immaterial, as she had no intention of allowing the deserters to live once the task was performed, she continued, "Naturally, I haven't anything in writing from him to prove this, but my backer is—!"

Before the brunette could falsely ascribe the support to Major General Benjamin Franklin Butler, a Radical Republican politician-turned-soldier known to oppose the Lincoln administration and who, being of higher rank, might be regarded as more "important" than Buller, there was an interruption.

While approaching the farm, Mary had taken precautions against being followed. She had left Martin Blick half a mile away to keep watch upon the trail leading to the Washington road and had instructed her third adherent to patrol around the building in case anybody should manage to pass without him raising the alarm.

"Who're y—?" Eric Lubbock commenced, the second word turning into a cry of agony, from close to the front of the house.

Grabbing at his revolver, alarm causing him to move swiftly yet in an ill-advised fashion, Graham swung around and wrenched open the front door. Before he could go through, he sprang aside. Hands clutching at the hilt of a knife that was protruding from his chest, Lubbock stumbled across the threshold and crumpled facedown on the floor. As he was going down, footsteps pounded hurriedly along the porch.

Snarling, startled curses burst from the deserters, and springing from where they sat at the table, each reached for the Army Colt—with which they had insisted upon being supplied by Mary—tucked into his waistband.

Despite wearing the *épée de combat* and taking pride in her skill at using it, the brunette made no attempt to draw it from its sheath. Instead, silently blessing the precaution she had taken of crossing the room to place the deserters between herself and Graham before starting the discussion, she turned to jerk open the door of the kitchen and went through without waiting to learn the identity of the newcomers. The way in which Lubbock was silenced warned they were unlikely to be police who had learned of and come to arrest the deserters. Every instinct she possessed suggested they were more than just robbers, so she concluded discretion the better part of valor and elected to make good her escape regardless of what befell her fellow conspirators.

With that thought in mind, showing a coolness Graham would have been advised to employ, the brunette closed and bolted the door behind her. As she ran to the side entrance, she heard the crash of shots from the sitting room. Hoping that neither deserter nor any of her adherents survived to implicate her, she unfastened the door. Drawing it cautiously open, she slid the sword from its sheath and left the house. Stepping as quietly as she could manage, she hurried toward the lean-to by

the barn, where her party had left their horses. A sigh of relief
came involuntarily as she discovered the intruders had not left
a guard on the animals. Replacing the weapon, she unfastened
her bay gelding. Leading it from the shelter, she mounted and
set off at a gallop.

Each carrying a shotgun with the barrels cut down to about
eighteen inches, held in a position of readiness, three figures
rapidly entered the sitting room in a loose arrowhead formation
that prevented any of them impeding another's line of fire. In
the lead was a burly man clad in the uniform of a Union soldier, and a second, wearing clothing suggesting he was employed in some form of sedentary occupation, was at the right.
While the last of the trio also wore masculine attire, the open-
necked black shirt, matching riding breeches, and Hessian
boots exhibited beyond doubt the wearer was a slender, bareheaded, and beautiful young woman with boyishly cropped
short black hair. Like her companions, she had a sidearm on
her person. In her case, it was an ivory-handled Dance Bros.
Navy revolver—a Confederate manufacturer's copy of the Colt
Navy Model of 1855—in the open-topped low-cavalry twist-
draw holster on the right side of a western-style gunbelt.

Receiving word of the plot to assassinate President Abraham
Lincoln, Mrs. Amy Cutler and Belle Boyd had agreed that the
attempt should be foiled at once. Each was sufficient of a realist
to accept that the Confederate States were unlikely to avoid
defeat, and they realized such an act, apparently by Southrons,
would arouse animosity to so great a pitch throughout the
North only an unconditional surrender, accompanied by reprisals of a virulent nature, would be acceptable to the Union. The
madam's excellent sources of information had already alerted
her to the connection between Mary Wilkinson and the deserters. Indiscreet remarks by the latter when paying a clandestine
visit to a low-priced brothel had suggested where they were
being hidden.

Given the services of two competent and trustworthy male
agents, the Rebel Spy had planned her campaign. Although

born in the North, each held to the Southron belief that any state finding its policies at odds with those of the federal government should be allowed to secede from the Union, a major cause of the war, so were serving the Confederate states against their own people. Supplied with horses by the soldier, having reverted to her natural hair color and washed away the body stain, Belle and her companions had followed the brunette's party without being detected. A skilled hunter, despite his sedentary occupation as clerk in the army's Medical Department, the civilian had killed the first of the lookouts in silence. Being compelled to rely upon a throw instead of thrusting the weapon home by hand, he had failed to prevent the dying Eric Lubbock from giving warning of their presence. However, to counteract this, the door to the farmhouse had been opened for them.

Even as Kendall was liberating the Army Colt from his belt, the soldier halted just clear of where Lubbock had fallen and opened fire. Held just above waist level, the shotgun bellowed twice in very rapid succession. There was no need for careful aim. Instinctive alignment was sufficient at such close quarters. Starting to spread as they left the twin cut-down ten-gauge barrels, eighteen .32-caliber buckshot balls engulfed and swept the shorter deserter from his feet, although not all of them hit him in the torso.

Showing what some people would have considered an even greater competence, the more slender and clerkly-looking civilian discharged his weapon a fraction of a second after that of his male companion. However, he restricted himself to a single chamber load. This proved sufficient. Before Blunkett could complete lining the revolver he was holding, he too was caught in a spray of soft lead balls and went sprawling lifeless to the floor.

Finding himself confronted by a young woman, who seemed vaguely familiar, gave Graham the courage to respond after the fashion of a cornered rat. Spitting out vile obscenities in a voice high with something close to hysteria, he thrust forward the Colt he had drawn and cocked involuntarily. For all his seemingly advantageous position, as he started to snatch at the trigger, he was to fare no better than either of the deserters.

Swinging her borrowed shotgun with the deft speed of much training, Belle depressed the forward trigger by a smooth squeeze instead of the frightened jerk being employed against her. Her wiry strength notwithstanding, the savage recoil caused by only one powder charge rocked her onto her heels and the barrels were tilted toward the ceiling with a force beyond her control. However, fortunately for her, this happened an instant after the load had cleared the muzzle and it was not deflected.

The young man was so close, the nine balls had not separated to any great extent when all of them ploughed into the center of his chest. He was literally picked up and thrown backward, and the barrel of his revolver was jolted aside as its hammer was falling. When it barked, it was no longer in alignment upon its intended target. The margin was small, but proved to be just enough. Passing through the material where the raised right sleeve joined the bodice of the black shirt, the bullet went by the girl without touching flesh.

"Where's the Wilkinson woman?" the civilian asked, glancing around the sitting room through the wafting clouds of powder smoke.

"I saw that door over there closing as we came in!" the soldier replied. Throwing a quick look at the shotgun, he dropped it and reached for the flap of his military pattern holster, going on, "God damn it, I'm empty!"

"Have mine and don't take chances just because she's a woman!" Belle instructed, holding forward the smoking weapon. "There's still one load in it, but I used the other!"

Accepting the shotgun, the soldier ran across the room. Finding the door fastened, he lowered his left shoulder and charged to burst it open. About to follow the men into the kitchen, Belle heard the drumming of hooves outside the building. She and her companions had seen the horses in the lean-to

while approaching the farmhouse on foot, but had decided
against doing anything to prevent them from being used for an
escape. By sheer bad luck, the omission was offering the brunette a means of fleeing.

11

I've No Fat Blonde to Help Me

"Wilkinson's riding off!" Belle Boyd called, spinning around to leap over the body of Alister Graham and running out the front door of the farmhouse with the civilian on her heels.

"Missed, God damn it!" the man growled, having brought up and fired the second load from his shotgun after the rapidly departing brunette.

"No chance of getting her with a handgun, either!" the Rebel Spy estimated, making no attempt to draw her Dance Bros. Navy revolver. Instead, she started to sprint toward the lean-to, continuing, "But we mustn't let *her* of all of them get away!"

Although Belle and her companions had followed Mary Wilkinson's party on horseback until approaching her destination, it had not been possible to ride all the way. Instead, they had left the animals hitched to a bush while dealing with Martin Blick and closed in upon their quarry on foot.

Entering the lean-to, the Rebel Spy studied the remaining horses. The conclusions she drew, based upon her considerable experience in matters equestrian, were not encouraging. Neither animal was what she would have regarded as top quality. They were, in fact, the kind of mounts hired by livery barns to customers who knew no better than to accept them, or were not too choosy over what was ridden.

Hoping the brunette was no better mounted, Belle unfastened what her instincts suggested would prove the better horse. Before the civilian had reached the lean-to, she was mounted and setting the animal into motion. Although she was still able to see her departing quarry, she knew the chase would be long and its outcome anything except certain. Nevertheless, she had no intention of giving up the pursuit. As she had told her companion, of all the conspirators, Mary Wilkinson was the one they could not leave alive. If this was done, the brunette might find other assistants and continue the attempt to have President Abraham Lincoln assassinated.

One thing soon became obvious to the Rebel Spy.

There was so little to choose between the two horses that the outcome would depend upon the relative ability of the riders.

Making an assessment as the pursuit continued, Belle felt confident she had the edge. While the brunette was a competent horsewoman, she had never before found reason to ride with her life at stake. On the other hand, there had been several occasions when only skill and daring—acquired in part when she had accompanied her father and male neighbors on fox hunts across rough country before the war—had saved the Rebel Spy from being captured by the Yankees. What was more, she was lighter and, possessing superior ability, could get more out of her mount.

Glances taken to the rear warned Belle that, as she had suspected, the civilian was unable to keep up with her. A city dweller, despite his capability as a hunter and stalker of human beings, his use as an agent for the South lay in other directions. Not that she cared. Regardless of her duty in the matter, having heard what had been said by the brunette about her in her character of "Françoise," she wanted to settle accounts with Mary personally. What was more, although the distance be-

tween herself and the brunette was decreasing noticeably as
they drew away from the man, she realized the chase must be
ended before they came too close to any other human habita-
tion. The farmhouse was sufficiently removed from its nearest
neighbors for the shooting to have gone unheard, but this
would not be the case if the pursuit was protracted.

"*Mademoiselle* Wilkinson!" the Rebel Spy called, employing
the accent used while being "Françoise" and projecting her
voice in the way she had learned on the hunting fields of Louisiana, "I've no fat blonde to help me now, so why do you run
away?"

While the words reached her with complete clarity, it was a
few seconds before their import struck the brunette. Looking
over her shoulder, she let out a hiss of surprise, which turned to
fury as she recognized that her pursuer—the civilian being out
of sight in the woodland through which the chase was now
taking place—was the slender "French Canadian" girl who had
soundly beaten her in their fight. Prudence should have dictated that she keep going, but prudence was something she only
rarely employed. Without even waiting until she could make
sure "Françoise" was alone, she started to turn her horse and to
draw the Navy Colt from its holster on the pommel of her
saddle.

Shrieking out a profanity, Mary sent her mount to meet the
approaching rider. As she did so, it seemed "Françoise" was
having second thoughts about repeating her challenge. Instead
of advancing to meet the charge, or showing any sign that she
was even carrying a weapon, the "redhead" was slowing her
horse. Wondering if "Françoise" was expecting them to fight
with bare hands, the brunette decided she was going to pay
dearly for the error if this should be the case. Despite the fact
that "Françoise" was unable to see the gunbelt and its holstered
revolver from her position, Mary Wilkinson felt no greater a
compunction over what she was intending to do than when she
had offered to wrestle at the dinner party given by George
Wigg, intending to attack an—she had assumed—unsuspecting
and harmless victim.

Thrusting forward and cocking the Navy Colt, Mary lined it at the slender figure she was approaching and squeezed off a shot. Immediately, she discovered that such an act was ill advised under the circumstances. Although she had used the weapon regularly enough to have achieved reasonable competence, this was the first occasion she had fired from the back of a horse. Nor was the animal between her legs used to having a firearm discharged from so close to its head. Instantly, it gave notice of its alarm by squealing in terror and throwing itself into a rearing swing away from the offending sound. Acting more on the instincts acquired at riding than by conscious thought, Mary managed to grab hold of the pommel with both hands and, at the cost of allowing the revolver to fly from her grasp, was able to remain astride the saddle. For a few seconds her full attention was occupied in regaining some semblance of control over the badly frightened animal. When this was achieved, she found that to all appearances fortune was favoring her.

By pure chance, the bullet fired at Belle had hit her horse in the head.

Although the Rebel Spy had almost halted the animal, she had not fired, suspecting that to use her Dance from its back would produce the same kind of response experienced by the brunette. But she was unable to free her feet from the stirrup irons as the horse collapsed. In going down onto its right side, it caught her leg beneath it. Pain seared through the trapped limb, but she was granted a few seconds vitally required respite by the way in which her assailant's mount was behaving. Only the leg was giving indication of injury, but she was able to visualize the gravity of her situation. Not merely to visualize, but to try to counteract it. Liberating her left foot, she placed it on the seat of the saddle and shoved with all the strength she could muster. Unfortunately, even though only the right ankle and foot were pinned, the dead weight of the horse was far too great for her to free herself in such a fashion.

Looking at the trapped girl, Mary realized the advantage she was being offered by her lucky shot and she almost flung herself from the saddle in her eagerness to make the most of it. Glancing around, she discovered her Navy Colt had landed on soft ground into which its muzzle was buried. Concluding the barrel would in all probability be so badly plugged it would need cleaning before a shot could be sent through it in safety, she was not perturbed. It would, she decided, be vastly more satisfying to kill the "redhead" with cold steel.

"I don't know why you got into this, you pox-riddled scraggy-gutted tail-peddler!" the brunette declared, drawing satisfaction from watching the ineffectual attempts of her intended victim to get free from the dead animal as she swept the *épée de combat* out of its sheath and swaggered forward. "But this is as far as you go!"

"Is it?" Belle asked, stopping the nonproductive shoving and bringing the Dance from beneath her.

Cupping her left hand around the right for added support, the Rebel Spy rested both wrists on the saddle. While taking aim with the aid of the rudimentary sights, she thumb-cocked the hammer. Flame erupted in a glowing muzzle flash as she squeezed the trigger. Despite the pain being caused to her trapped lower leg and the awkward firing position, she held true.

Savoring the thought of how she would take her revenge, Mary appreciated her own peril a fraction of a second too late. Flying upward at an angle, the .36-caliber soft round ball ejected through the seven-and-three-eighths-inch-long barrel of the Dance entered beneath her chin. Driven onward through the brain, it was halted by the roof of the skull. Halted in her tracks and killed instantly, she nevertheless remained standing for a moment. Then, the *épée* slipping from her lifeless grasp, she toppled slowly, as if reluctantly, backward.

"You're one person I don't regret killing, Wilkinson!" Belle breathed, realizing she would have no need to take further action to protect herself from the brunette and had removed one threat to the life of President Lincoln.

"Thank god you're all right, Miss Boyd!" the civilian exclaimed, riding up a few seconds later and starting to dismount.

"I couldn't make this goddamned plug run fast enough to keep up, and though I saw what was happening, I was still too far off to be able to help."

"I guessed that was what happened," Belle admitted truthfully. "But I got her anyway. Can you help me free my leg, please?"

"It isn't broken!" the civilian announced, after having contrived to move the dead horse sufficiently for the Rebel Spy to be able to withdraw her foot and remove the boot to examine it. "But it's so badly sprained you'll not be walking on it for a few days."

"Damn it!" Belle gasped. "We've settled Wilkinson and her cronies, but Buller still has to be stopped."

"Then somebody else will have to do it," the civilian declared.[1]

1. The injury ended the participation of Belle "the Rebel Spy" in the affairs of Brigadier General Moses J. Buller. However, as word still had not reached Washington, District of Columbia, about the outcome of the assignment, by the time she recovered, she went to Arkansas with the results recorded in: *The Colt and the Saber* and *The Rebel Spy*. J. T. E.

12

He's Charged With Cowardice

"All right, you men!" Captain Dustine Edward Marsden ("Dusty") Fog called, running his gaze over the dozen soldiers who were standing before him, each about to load his Colt 1860 Army revolver. "Make sure you only put a quarter of a charge in the chambers!"

"A goddamned *quarter* of a son-of-a-bitching charge is it?" muttered a newly arrived recruit, glancing from his weapon to its powder flask, and regarding the task to which he was currently assigned as far short of what he had believed he would be doing when he had enrolled. "Why the hell're we fooling around this way, 'stead of getting out and fighting the Yankees?"

"You're doing it 'cause Cap'n Dusty wants it doing that way," Sergeant Kiowa Cotton announced, stepping closer to the speaker. He had heard the sotto voce comment, as its maker intended he should, believing that he would share the sentiment.

"Now, that don't seem like too all fired good a reason to *me!*" the enlisted man declared, glancing at the soldiers on either side of him to ensure they were being made aware of his salty toughness. "I ain't *never* loaded less'n full, 'cepting when I was knee-high to a horny-toad."

"You do what you want," Kiowa drawled, having come across a similar mentality many times. "Only, happen you've a mind to load her with *more* 'n that said quarter charge, was I you, there's something I'd do first off."

"What'd that be?"

"Go take that old Colt to the armorer. Have him file off the foresight knob, hammer spur 'n' triggerguard, then take out the trigger to boot."

"Now, why'd I do a thing like *that?*"

" 'Cause," the sergeant explained, his Indian-dark features savage in their cold mockery, "happen you do cut loose with more'n said quarter charge and spoil any of those hosses for shooting off their backs, Cap'n Dusty'll take your goddamned Army Colt and ram it clear up your butt!"

"You reckon he could do it?" the enlisted man inquired, trying to make the words sound like a challenge, as he remembered all he had heard about the commanding officer of Company C since his arrival at the headquarters of the Texas Light Cavalry. He was impressed, in spite of himself, by the vehemence with which the grim-visaged noncom had addressed him.

"Soldier, I don't just *reckon,*" Kiowa asserted. "I flat out know for *certain* he could do it. One-handed and leftie to boot."

"Him?" the enlisted man almost yelped, finding it difficult to reconcile the reputation acquired by Captain Dusty Fog with his far from impressive physical appearance.

"You mind Cy Bollinger?"

"That blacksmith jasper? Sure, I've seed him around."

"Big *hombre,* ain't he?" Kiowa hinted.

"Big's I've seed, even back home to San Saba County," the soldier conceded after a moment of thought, employing the air of one conferring a favor. "Which means they don't come a whole heap bigger no other place."

"Likely," Kiowa grunted dryly. "Well I mind one time, just afore Cap'n Dusty got made captain, he got to wondering same way's you. He got whupped so fast he must've thought the hawgs'd jumped him."[1]

"How'd a short-growed kid do that to a feller his size?" the enlisted man asked, being too prudent for all his bombast to phrase his doubts in any other fashion.

"You've seed Tommy Okasi around?"

"That lil Chinee jasper's fetches 'n' carries for Ole Devil?"

"That's him," Kiowa agreed, without demanding that the correct title of General Jackson Baines ("Ole Devil") Hardin should be used by the recruit. " 'Cepting he allows to hail from some place name of Japan, not China. Well, he's taught Cap'n Dusty some fancy wrassling tricks the like of which I've never seed. Neither'd Cy nor any of those other big fellers's made the same goddamned stupid mistake where he's concerned."

"Sergeant Cotton!" called the subject of the discussion. "If you pair could put off talking for a spell, the rest of us would like to get on with what we're here for!"

"Yo!" the Indian-dark noncom responded, noticing the enlisted man was starting to charge the chambers of his Army Colt with the required amount of black powder.

Although the recruit was not a member of Company C, he had been sent to help in a task assigned to its commanding officer. The work at present being undertaken explained why the horses ridden during the raid on the bridge over the Mushogen River had been better behaved under fire than the mounts of the New Hampstead Volunteers.

Having been "three-saddled" before delivery to the Texas

---

1. A later and more amicable encounter between Dustine Edward Marsden "Dusty" Fog and Cyrus "Cy" Bollinger is described in: Part One, "The Schoolteacher," *The Hard Riders* and, revised in the light of information supplied to us by Alvin Dustine "Cap" Fog, its "expansion," *Master of Triggernometry*. J. T. E.

Light Cavalry,[2] a recently arrived batch of remounts were being conditioned to accept having firearms discharged by their riders. It was a lengthy process, made possible only by having such a good supply of horses that the newcomers could be "brought on" before allocating them for duty in the field, therefore making them reliable when taken into action.

After having had a firearm placed in the manger with its feed, allowing it to become familiar with the sight and smell of the alien object, the horse was next accustomed to the sound of the action being operated while unloaded. With this accomplished, while being ridden, it was shown the weapon sometimes presented to the front and one side or the other of its head. When it had become reconciled to the sight, it was subjected to having first a single, then a succession of percussion caps discharged from its back. Having accepted this, it was subjected to a growing charge of powder augmenting the cap until willing to accept the crack of a full load. If at any stage of the proceedings it showed signs of being uneasy over what was taking place, it would be walked for a short while and petted until calmed down.

Watching the response of the horses carefully as the revolvers were discharged with no greater noise than he had ordered, Dusty nodded his approval. At his side, Sergeant Major Billy Jack expressed a similar satisfaction by remarking that all the lack of protesting reaction proved was that they had been given a bunch of stone-deaf crow-bait likely to fall dead should it become necessary to walk slowly for more than a few feet.

"Walk them a spell, then, and make sure you didn't overcall how far they'd last," the small Texan told his apparently pessimistic subordinate. "Happen I'm lucky, one of them will fall on you."

2. A professional "bronc buster" in Texas considered a horse to be sufficiently broken for use after he had "saddled," ridden, it three times. All further training was the responsibility of the cowhand into whose possession it came. J. T. E.

"It'll more likely be every last son of a bitch of 'em," the sergeant major corrected. "Company A's coming in."

"Looks like they've had some luck," Dusty remarked, turning his gaze to the double column of men riding toward the training area.

"*They* allus do," Billy Jack claimed, his demeanor so dismal a stranger would have believed Company C met with nothing except disaster and misfortune.

"Cousin Pete doesn't have a calamity wailer like *you* as his topkick," Dusty pointed out with well-simulated asperity.

"There ain't only the one like *me*," the sergeant countered. "Which, maybe Cap'n Blaze don't have *all* the luck that's going 'round."

"If having *you* around's lucky," the small Texan asserted, "I'm going to start breaking mirrors and stomping black cats!"

"My momma always used to do that," Billy Jack drawled with doleful satisfaction. "Which's how I got the way I am."

Having made the comment, the lanky sergeant major ambled rather than marched off to carry out his orders. However, there was nothing of his seeming hangdog misery in the way he addressed the enlisted men. Nor, knowing his true nature and capabilities, did any of them delay before obeying the orders he gave.

"Howdy, Cousin Dusty," greeted Captain Peter Blaze, who looked like a somewhat older and less reckless version of the small Texan's second-in-command. Signaling for the man by his side to accompany him, he reined his clearly hard-ridden mount clear of his company and, halting, went on, "Come on over and meet Lieutenant Frank Dailey of the Third U.S. Cavalry. Mr. Dailey, let me present Captain Fog!"

"My pleasure, si—!" the young man in the Union blue uniform began, stiffening instinctively into a formal brace, despite his understandable air of dejection. Then an appreciation of what he had heard struck home, and staring at the small figure walking briskly forward, he gasped, "Captain *Dusty* Fog?"

"There's only the one Captain Fog in the Texas Light Cavalry, mister," Pete Blaze said dryly, although he was far from surprised by the response to his introduction. "Which, some have said, is more than enough."

"We're awful long on Blazes, though, even if only two of them've made captain," Dusty commented, no more surprised by the reaction of the Yankee than his cousin and, having grown accustomed to such emotions, feeling not the slightest animosity over its being displayed. "Fact being, here comes another of them!"

Looking from one to the other Texan, Dailey sensed their banter was—in part, at least—being carried out to try and relieve some of the misery which was assailing him. If such was the case, he concluded, it was in keeping with the chivalrous conduct which he had frequently heard, and now witnessed at first hand, was accorded by their regiment to those who fell into their clutches. Certainly he had no complaint about the treatment given to those of his men wounded when he had led them into an ambush. What was more, while he alone was taken along as a prisoner, he had been subjected to no humiliation or abuse.

However, thinking of something other than his personal misfortunes, the young Yankee lieutenant devoted the majority of his attention to the smaller of the Rebel captains. Recently promoted and sent to join a regiment though he might be, Dailey had the natural instinct of a professional soldier for recognizing a born leader. Short, almost insignificant to the eye at first glance, Dusty Fog was worthy of his rank. Although he too, could be classed as a volunteer who had entered his country's army to serve in its present conflict, he was a vastly different proposition from those in a similar category on the Union's side in Arkansas. Here was no wealthy young dandy enrolled for the prestige of an officer's uniform, nor middle-class "liberal" snob dripping smug patronage while despising as poorly educated morons the enlisted men placed under his command. Here was one with the capability of earning the respect of those under his orders. He obviously did not require the authority vested by the *Manual of Field Regulations* to ensure he was obeyed.

Coming up at something approaching a run, saber bouncing on its slings from his waist belt and face a trifle flushed under the constraining clutch of an unaccustomed closed collar and cravat, the arrival of First Lieutenant Charles William Henry ("Red") Blaze diverted the attention of the captured Yankee from Dusty. Being officer of the day, Red was obliged to discard his comfortable skirtless tunic and bandana, replacing them with the attire laid down in the *Manual of Dress Regulations*. Skidding to a halt, he snapped into a brace and threw up a salute divided equally between his older brother—one of twins—and his cousin.

"Take charge of Mr. Dailey, please, Red," Pete requested.

"Yo!" the officer of the day assented. "You might as well get down, friend; it's not far to my tent and we'll bed you down there for the night."

"Thank you," Dailey replied, obeying. However, as he dismounted, he swung his gaze to the small Texan and, feeling not the least awkward or surprised at addressing an enemy in such a formal fashion, went on, "Excuse me, Captain Fog, sir!"

"Yes, mister?" Dusty inquired, noticing the urgency in which the Yankee had spoken to him.

"It was you who blew up the Mushogen Bridge, wasn't it?" Dailey asked.

"My company helped more than a smidgin," the small Texan replied.

"You've made such a mess of it, heavy transport still can't get over," Dailey declared, with a frankness he hoped might serve his purpose. "There's to be a court martial because of it."

"That figures," Dusty drawled, surprised at the bitterness which had come into the lieutenant's voice during the second sentence. Yet a professional soldier such as he appeared to be should have expected the officer commanding the ineffective guard to be court-martialed. Then he remembered something else and went on, "I thought you said you killed the major you suckered into chasing after you, Red?"

"Things being what they were, I didn't stop to hold a mirror in front of his mouth and make certain sure," the freckle-faced

Rebel lieutenant replied. "But, going by the hole 'tween his eyes, I surely figured he was dead."

"He was killed all right," Dailey declared.

"Then who're they court-martialing?" Dusty asked.

"Kirby Cogshill," Dailey answered, his face flushed with anger.

"Who-all might he be?" the small Texan inquired.

"The lieutenant who was second-in-command of the guard detail," the Yankee officer supplied, sensing the interest his words were arousing and hoping he would learn something to justify a belief he—along with others like him—had formed with regards to the matter under discussion. "The one you wounded."

"That one, huh?" Dusty said quietly, face creasing with a frown. "But how the hell can he be court-martialed?"

"He's charged with cowardice in the face of the enemy," Dailey explained. "They've added dereliction of duty, failing to obey an order given by a superior, and deserting his command. Any and all of which carry the death penalty, Captain Fog. They say he left his men and ran away from the fighting."

Hardly believing their ears, the small Texan and his cousin exchanged looks. It was Dusty who spoke, his voice hard and angry:

"That's a damned lie! The lieutenant was the only one of them who made any attempt at doing his duty correctly. In the first place, he wanted to search the bushes where Kiowa and I, that's my sergeant scout, were hidden, but the major was set on moving out even though their relief wasn't there yet. Then he went after them when they chased off after Red and our boys, hoping to stop them because he guessed what was likely coming. Only he looked back, saw us, and turned to try and stop us from setting the charges and blowing the bridge."

"And that's how he told it," Dailey stated. "But the major who made all the mistakes was General Buller's brother."

"So *that's* the way of it!" the blond Texan breathed, and gently as he spoke, the Yankee lieutenant ceased to think of him as being small.

"That's the way of it, sir," Dailey confirmed, but loyalty to a respected superior made him continue, despite a disinclination to wash the dirty linen of his service in the presence of enemies. "The way things are, Colonel McDonald has had no choice but to order the court martial convened. Buller's sergeant major and a corporal laid the accusation, and as there aren't any other witnesses, it's their word against that of Kirby."

"There were other witnesses, mister!" Dusty corrected. "Kiowa and I saw and heard most of what happened."

"Billy Jack and I saw the lieutenant following his men until he saw you and turned back, Dusty," Red supplemented.

"But there's no way any of you could give evidence," Dailey protested. "Is there?"

"I don't know," the small Texan admitted. "But should there be, I'll bet Uncle Devil knows and will fix it for us."

13

I Want the Bastard Found *Guilty*

"God damn that interfering Scotch son of a bitch!" Brigadier General Moses J. Buller snarled, neither knowing nor caring that the racial classification should have been "Scottish." Glaring furiously at the more bulky of the two men standing before the folding table in the big wall tent which circumstances were forcing him to use instead of having reached the comfortable accommodation at his headquarters, he went on, "Are you sure he's going through with it?"

"He sure is, bo—*General*," Sergeant Major Alden Packard confirmed nervously, concluding he was correct in his belated suspicion that the news he had taken it upon himself to deliver would be far from welcomed by its recipient. "As soon as that son-of-a-bitching luff of his, Dailey, got back and told him about it, he started making arrangements for that goddamned Reb officer and two noncom's blowed up the bridge out there to come 'n' give their evidence at Cogshill's court martial. They're likely fixing to come to Mushogen and do it right now."

"Why the hell did Mick Meacher let him do it?" Buller demanded. "I told him to watch out for things while I was away.
Didn't he try to stop the son of a bitch?"

"I dunno," Packard answered untruthfully, having heard
that Colonel Michael ("Fatso") Meacher had made an unsuccessful attempt to dissuade Colonel Iain McDonald of the
Third Cavalry from accepting the offer of evidence on behalf of
First Lieutenant Kirby Cogshill made by the commanding general of the Confederate Army of Arkansas and North Texas.

"There was no way he could stop it," Major Saul Montreigen
put in, less from a desire for fair play than to air a knowledge of
military matters which was greater than that of his superior.
Showing no sign of being put out by the baleful glare turned his
way, he went on, "It's a matter of seniority. McDonald was a
chicken colonel long before Meacher joined the army."

"May hell's fires burn the Scotch son of a bitch!" Buller spat
out, who was aware of the point raised by his subordinate and
suspected why it had been made. "Can he let those Rebel bastards come and do it?"

"I expect he'll be able to quote precedents for it," the slim
major answered, the query having been directed at him. "I suppose all the negotiations were carried out under a flag of truce,
but I can't understand how the Rebs heard what was going
on."

"Dailey'd got took prisoner," Packard supplied, as both officers looked his way. "Seems they turned him loose with the
word when he told them about Cogshill. That's why I come out
here to meet you, General. I figured you'd want to know what's
doing as soon's possible."

"I'd a goddamned sight sooner you'd come and told me
something's being done about the son-of-a-bitching thing!" the
general asserted, glowering unpleasantly at the junior of his
subordinates and speaking with savage bitterness. "Because I
want the bastard found *guilty*!"

As the response indicated, the attempt at ingratiation on the
part of the burly sergeant major was failing to produce the
results he had hoped for.

What Packard had not taken into account until it was too late for him to withdraw was that bearers of bad news are never welcome.

Under the prevailing circumstances, in fact, the information delivered by the sergeant major was only adding to what his superior regarded as having been—with only one possible and one positive exception—a most unsatisfactory sequence of events.

Apart from the excellent ministrations he had received at the hands of Thaddeus Barnes and the possibilities suggested by the deadly liquid David Aaranovitch had produced, but which still had to be proved capable of doing what was claimed of it, the general regarded the visit he had paid to Washington as having been closer to a disaster than the triumph he had sought to attain in more than one field of activity.

Not only had Buller been refused the extra troops and more modern equipment he had requested from the general staff, but there had been broad hints that his conduct—or rather his lack of any positive action—since assuming command in Arkansas was far from being regarded favorably by the War Department. It had been made clear to him that his current rank would be in jeopardy if there was no improvement in the situation. While remaining a brigadier general—or even attaining advancement —meant nothing to him on a military basis, either would offer benefits when the war was over. On the other hand, if it were to become known that he had been reduced to the rank of colonel —or even lower—for such reasons, it could have an equally adverse effect on the high ambitions he held for his return to civilian life. No door could be closed, not even those previously beyond his reach, to a man who came back acclaimed as a hero and successful campaign commander, but there were plenty of people who would be willing to use the excuse of his failure to keep him from their society.

The hopes nourished by Buller of acquiring political backing in the capital had proved no more fruitful. Only a few minutes in their company had warned him that, being alike only in their mutual devotion to self-interest, neither George Wigg nor Colonel Horace Trumpeter would be of use in helping his advancement. He drew some satisfaction, however, from the knowledge that he had deprived the former of a most efficient and competent butler. This had been one small source of consolation. Another was that, although his most illicit and potentially dangerous association had fizzled into nothing, his own involvement in what had amounted to high treason had remained undiscovered.

It had never been Buller's intention to remain in Washington until the proposed assassination of President Abraham Lincoln was attempted. He had meant to leave the supervision and, no matter what the result might be—having decided Mary Wilkinson would prove too dangerous an ally, regardless of her potential as a possible contender in fights—the silencing of all the conspirators when it was over to Montreigen. However, he had been unable to take his departure as soon as he had intended.

For once, Second Lieutenant Robert Cryer had carried out a duty without delay. He had already left the hotel by the time Buller had tried to recall him and give him revised orders for Montreigen. However, his diligence had not included traveling at the greatest possible speed. As a result of the leisurely way in which he delivered the message and returned, the major had already set out for Arkansas with Aaranovitch and their equipment before he reported to his superior. Nor had it been possible for him to go after Montreigen with the news of the change in arrangements, which had placed him in command of the escort, until the following morning. However, this had proved to be of no importance. Although the authorities had no idea how it happened, Buller had already heard that the badly charred bodies of five men had been found in a burned-out farmhouse north of the city.

Catching up with the remainder of his party, who had been telegraphed to await his coming, the general had devoted all his energies to speeding their return to his headquarters. He was helped in this by the excellent transportation system that had been extended westwards, although not actually into Arkansas, by the army. Traveling as far as possible on the railroad, the crossing of the Mississippi River being made by ferry boats designed to carry heavy transport, the later stages of the journey were in the well-guarded wagon train he had ordered.

However, it was not until Buller was almost there that he had heard about the destruction of the bridge over the Mushogen River. Aware that the incident might prove the final straw as far as the general staff was concerned, particularly as his brother was in command of the guard that failed to protect the vital link in communications, he had been delighted to hear a scapegoat was available to divert the blame from where it belonged. Handled properly, he had concluded, the court martial could be used to remove some of the pressure from him. Knowing the strong connections of the Cogshill family with the army's top brass, he believed they might be induced to lend him their support in return for his intervention to save the young lieutenant from the consequence of a verdict of guilty.

Everything depended upon such a verdict being returned.

The news brought by Packard threatened to dash all of Buller's hopes in that direction.

Knowing Colonel Iain McDonald of the Third Cavalry, a career soldier of some competence, the general did not doubt that the admission of evidence from the enemy officer and men would prove crucial. Although he had never admitted his suspicions, he was sure the events had not occurred as described by the sergeant major and Corporal John Silkin. In fact, he had believed Cogshill turned back to try and avert the disaster being caused by the stupid and ill-advised behavior of his brother.

"Getting a verdict of guilty ought to be easy enough," Montreigen commented in a dryly judicial fashion, eyeing the sergeant major sardonically. "There's only whatever evidence these Rebs can give to go against what Packard and Silkin *say* happened."

"Are you calling me a liar?" the bulky noncom growled indignantly.

"It doesn't matter one way or the other to me," the major pointed out, showing neither alarm nor concern over the

threatening manner displayed by the sergeant major. "But Mc-
Donald reckons you could be lying, or at best, mistaken."

"Shut your goddamned yapper!" Buller warned, as Packard
prepared to speak. "Is there *anything* they could say to make
liars of you and Silkin?"

"Who's going to believe a bunch of mother-something
Rebs?" the sergeant major growled sullenly, if evasively.

"I'd say that all depends on what *they* have to say," Montreigen guessed, before his superior could respond to Packard's
heated comment. "And which officers are sitting as judges in
the court."

"I'll damned soon see to *that!*" Buller claimed, coming to his
feet with a vigor that overturned his chair and nearly upset the
table.

"Not if they've already been picked out, which I'm betting
they will be," the major contradicted. "In fact, I'm willing to
lay money that McDonald's already let the top brass know
what's going on and *he'll* get backing from them."

"Against *me?*" the general asked, touching the insignia of
rank on the collar of a tunic that was far cleaner than had
previously been the case, as a result of the ministrations performed by Barnes. "I outrank any goddamned colonel!"

"On paper," Montreigen conceded. "But all those regular-
army bastards stand together, and they're not going to sit back
and let one of their own, which Cogshill is regardless of only
being a luff, go down if they think he's being railroaded by a
volunteer."

"Do you know what you're implying?" Buller challenged.

"I'm only telling you how it might look to *them,*" the major
answered, displaying no greater perturbation by the wrath directed his way by his superior than he had a few seconds earlier
from his subordinate. However, he swung around, right hand
reaching for the hilt of the *épée de combat* he carried instead of
a saber, as a soft footfall reached his ears. "What do y—!"

"I beg your pardon, General Buller, *sir,*" Thaddeus Barnes
intoned, rather than merely said, entering the wall tent as if
oblivious of everything except his employer. In some way, he

contrived to employ the honorific with a politeness and respect that made it clear he did not include the other two men present, which was most gratifying to its recipient. "I came to ask whether you are ready for dinner to be served, sir."

"Not just yet," Buller refused, delighted as was always the case by the treatment he was accorded by his butler. The deferential behavior of Barnes was so flattering to his ego, he had quickly ceased to wonder what had become of his much less satisfactory "striker" who had not put in an appearance since having failed to report for duty on the morning after the dinner party at George Wigg's mansion. "I'll send word when I want it."

"Very good, sir," the butler replied, as if approving of what he had been told. "I had anticipated a delay and have had a meal prepared that will not be spoiled by it."

"There's something about that smooth-talking son of a bitch I don't like!" Montreigen growled, watching the tall, slender and distinguished-looking, somberly attired man depart as unobtrusively as he had come, after having set up the overturned chair.

"He suits *me*!" the general declared, guessing the acrimonious comment was caused by the somehow polite lack of deference his butler invariably showed to the major. He had frequently been irritated by Montreigen's assumption of superiority in matters of etiquette and the social graces, so was far from averse to seeing the other treated with what was clearly indifference. "And you say that about almost everybody!"

"I learned early not to take *anybody* on trust," the major asserted, but decided against mentioning certain—fairly accurate, if he had realized—theories he had formed about the girl who had called herself "Françoise." "And, to my way of thinking, that soft-walking son of a bitch came to work for you a sight too eagerly."

"I'm paying him a whole lot better than that tight-butted skinflint Wigg," Buller pointed out. "And he's less work to do for his money."

"That would help," Montreigen admitted, paying no attention to the sour way in which his superior was looking at him. "Particularly if he's still drawing pay from Wigg for keeping an eye on you."

"Which is what he's doing," the general answered, his porcine features taking on an expression of triumphant satisfaction over being able to prove that his arrogant subordinate was drawing an erroneous conclusion. "He told me about it that afternoon when he came back from quitting Wigg and collecting his gear. He said that the grave-digging, corpse-robbing son of a bitch had given him money to be told about anything I got up to. Then he let me in on a few things Wigg wouldn't want known. I reckon he's trustworthy all right." Then swinging his gaze to his second subordinate in a way that indicated he considered nothing further needed saying on the subject, he continued with the briskness of one getting down to something of vastly greater importance. "What can you tell me about those goddamned Johnny Rebs McDonald's bringing in for the court martial, Packard?"

Returning to the side of the big wall tent from which he had moved when he had seen a soldier approaching, having had no desire to be caught eavesdropping, Thaddeus Barnes listened to the reply given by the sergeant major. What he heard, added to the ensuing conversation, suggested a means by which he might complete his real purpose for entering the employment of Brigadier General Buller.

As in the case of "Françoise," the doubts aroused in Major Montreigen by the butler were justified.

Having expressed sentiments similar to those of the two men who worked to remove the threat to the life of President Lincoln, in addition to being most competent in his work, Barnes had proved to be an exceptionally efficient member of the Confederate Secret Service. Making use of the opportunities granted by the nature of his employment, he had produced much useful information and had operated in conjunction with Mrs. Amy Cutler. Alerted to the possibility of dissidents trying

to remove the President by assassination if need be, they had
decided this must be circumvented. While he had gone to work
for George Wigg with such an intention, he had seen how it
might also be possible to discover the nature of the work being
carried out for Buller by David Aaranovitch. Knowing the unusual diversion favored by the general, he had suggested this
offered a chance for Belle Boyd to gain Buller's confidence and
he had persuaded Wigg to supply the "entertainment" that had
brought this about.

Waiting outside the hotel to receive the Rebel Spy's report,
Barnes had accompanied her back to the brothel as they had
realized that the killing of First Lieutenant Martin Blick would
prevent her from continuing her assignment. Consulting with
the madam, it had been decided the matter was so important
that he must try to replace Belle in the general's entourage.
They had been helped to achieve their purpose by Buller's disinclination to spend money on things he considered unimpor-
tant. Instead of paying for accommodation in the servants'
quarters at the hotel, he had had his striker stay at the nearest
barracks. Waylaying the soldier as he was on his way to work,
disguised in a suitable fashion, Belle had lured him away and
rendered him unconscious with a drugged drink. On his recov-
ery in the middle of the afternoon, he had been informed that
he was listed as a deserter, and as he was disenchanted with the
living conditions as a member of the New Hampstead Volunteers, even for one in his employment, he had been only too
willing to accept the suggestion made by the Rebel Spy and flee
from Washington.

Knowing Buller would be suffering from the aftereffects of a
similar potion administered by Belle as a means of avoiding his
attentions, and delivering her report, Barnes had to time his
arrival at the hotel, and he was ready to put to use his knowledge of treating such a condition. He had had a letter from
Wigg to deliver and he came upon the scene when the stimulant
was most appreciated. After that, all had gone as required.

Learning of the arrangements being made between Mary
Wilkinson and Buller, via the use of a glass tumbler as an

extemporized listening device, Barnes had used the need to collect his belongings from Wigg's mansion as an excuse to warn his associates. By doing so, he had enabled the Rebel Spy and the two male agents to remove the threat to President Lincoln. However, he had been less successful in his primary objective. Despite having come as prepared as possible, he had been unable to find an opportunity to destroy the terrible liquid.

At the conclusion of the conversation, Barnes left the shadows thrown by the wall tent and into which his black suit, the jacket drawn across to conceal his white shirt, had blended admirably. As he was walking away, he looked about him so as to be sure he had fixed the layout of the camp on the northern bank of the Mushogen River firmly in his mind. Based upon what he had overheard, he believed he might have found a way by which the destruction he required could be brought about. Regardless of the unflattering comments made by Packard, if only a part of the stories concerning the man named as the "Johnny Reb officer" were true, he would have a most useful accomplice for the vitally important task.

However, being aware of the code of honor with which Southrons of his class were instilled during their formative years, the butler suspected there would be great difficulty in persuading Captain Dustine Edward Marsden Fog of the Texas Light Cavalry to do what would be required of him.

14
I'm Asking You to Break
Your Word

"May I help you, *sir?*"

At the first word, recognizing the polite yet somehow disrespectful voice he had come to know and resent, Major Saul Montreigen spun around from where he was examining the contents of the portmanteau he had placed on the bed. Seeing two officers who were not members of the New Hampstead Volunteers standing behind its owner at the now open front entrance of the wedge tent, he returned the almost drawn *épée de combat* to the sheath on his belt's slings. If Thaddeus Barnes had been alone, or even accompanied by enlisted men over whom he could exert authority and compel to back up his story, he would have settled his doubts by thrusting home the sword and claiming he responded instinctively to what he had believed to be a thief coming from behind him.

"I thought I saw somebody sneaking out the back there," Montreigen lied, pointing to the flaps at the rear of the tent, having severed the fastenings on entering to provide just such an excuse. "But I reckoned I'd better make sure I had before I raised the alarm and disturbed the camp."

"Most *thoughtful* of you, sir," the butler intoned, his austere features and the timbre of the words giving no indication of whether or not he believed the explanation.

"It looks like I was right and somebody got in to rob you," the major claimed. "Is anything missing?"

"No, sir," Barnes replied, after having advanced to carry out a surprisingly perfunctory inspection of his property. "Everything is still here."

"Have you got any other baggage the feller could have gone through?" Montreigen inquired, glancing around the sparsely furnished wedge tent allocated by Brigadier General Moses J. Buller for his butler's temporary accommodation.

"No, sir," Barnes replied, with seeming gratitude for the interest being taken in his affairs although there was in fact as little veracity as there had been in the explanation for the presence of the major. "I have few needs."

"Shall I have the guard start a search for the man you saw?" inquired the senior of the officers at the entrance to the tent.

"There is no need to put them to such trouble on my account, sir," Barnes declared, before Montreigen—to whom the question was directed—could reply. Looking around and making the honorific sound respectful rather than a subtly disguised term of reproach. "Nothing has been taken. May I thank you for accompanying me to investigate."

"Think nothing of it," the officer instructed and walked away with his companion.

"You're a limey, aren't you?" Montreigen asked, instead of leaving the tent.

"A *limey*, sir?" the butler repeated, then nodded and went on, "Ah, yes, I understand. You are employing the colloquialism which refers to the long-established practice on British vessels of issuing the crew with lime juice as a means of preventing scurvy. Yes, sir. As you infer, I am an Englishman."

"Then how come you are working in Washington?"

"I accompanied my former employer, Sir Randolph Reeder,

to this country in my capacity of gentleman's personal gentleman, in sixty-one. However—and I trust you to treat this
disclosure with the utmost confidence, sir—I found his life-
style was not amicable to that I expect from my gentleman and
so was compelled to retire from his service."

"Huh huh!" Montreigen grunted noncommittally, impressed
as always by the, on the surface, respectful—albeit haughty—
demeanor of the man he was addressing. It put him in mind of
the treatment he had been accorded by senior servants in the
homes of the best families at New Orleans, serving as a subtle
reminder that he, too, was in their opinion no more than a
superior form of employee. Telling himself that he would learn
nothing to the detriment of Barnes, but really wishing to leave
the company of a person who could inspire such a sense of
social inferiority, he finished, "Well, if you're satisfied nothing's
been taken, I may as well be on my way."

"I beg your pardon, sir," the butler said, as the major took
his first step away from the bed, "but may I ask if you had a
reason for coming in *this* direction?"

"Hell, *yes!*" Montreigen admitted, having forgotten why he
had arrived at the tent and, finding it unoccupied, deciding to
see if he could confirm his doubts with regards to Barnes. "But
seeing that feller sneaking out took it clear from my mind!"

"That is most understandable, sir," the butler conceded, with
such an aura of sincerity he might have been expressing genuine commiseration. "Conditions of stress, or surprise, frequently have such an effect, I am given to understand."

"Yeah!" Montreigen growled. "Anyways, Buller says he's got
a coach across the river to take him to Mushogen in the morning and he wants you ready to go with him."

"Very good, sir," Barnes replied. "Perhaps, if you are returning to his company, you would be so kind as to tell *General*
Buller on my behalf that I will be awaiting his pleasure from
sunrise, unless he requires my presence still earlier."

"I'll do that," the major promised, but with bad grace, only
willing to leave the company of one who—his arrogance notwithstanding—filled him with a sense of insignificance. "But,

knowing him, you can bet he won't be ready to go any too early."

"I *never* make wagers, sir, nor do I consider it *my* place to express an opinion respecting the habits of my employer," the butler answered, the implication he contrived to impart on the word *my,* indicating he actually meant *your.* "May I wish you good evening, sir?"

"Yeah!" Montreigen assented and stalked from the tent in something clearly more akin to a retreat than the departure of a superior from the presence of a social inferior.

"Tut tut tut!" Barnes clicked, watching with a kind of well-bred sardonic amusement as the officer disappeared into the darkness. Then, lowering the flaps of the tent, he mused further as he crossed to replace the clothing removed from his trunk, "You may be a competent professional duelist and hired assassin, *Major* Montreigen, but you would not last two days if you tried to play the 'Great Game'[1] in Europe. However, I suppose one might derive some consolation from appreciating that your behavior indicates I am *not* under suspicion by *General* Buller."

Always a light sleeper, this trait was never more pronounced than when Captain Dustine Edward Marsden ("Dusty") Fog knew himself to be in a precarious situation.

Despite the way in which he and his two companions had been treated generally since crossing the Ouachita River into Union territory, having survived two what he felt sure were deliberate attempts to kill or severely injure him that day, the small Texan considered he was far from being safe and secure in his present location.

On having been admitted when his request for an urgent interview was delivered, despite General Jackson Baines ("Ole Devil") Hardin's being engaged in an important conference

1. "Great Game": the British term at that period for any form of spying or counter-espionage activity. J. T. E.

with another senior officer of the Confederate Army,[2] Dusty
had found himself justified in his assumption that aid would be
forthcoming. Agreeing that First Lieutenant Kirby Cogshill
must be cleared of the false charges, Ole Devil had set about
arranging for the evidence to be supplied with the thoroughness
that characterized his commanding of the Army of Arkansas
and North Texas. Ordering First Lieutenant Frank Dailey to be
released on parole, pending the exchange of a Confederate prisoner of equal rank, he had written a letter outlining the true
state of affairs and making his proposal for delivery to Colonel
Iain McDonald of the Third United States Cavalry.

Finding the information regarding the destruction of the
bridge over the Mushogen River to be much as he had suspected, the Scottish officer had applied all the experience acquired in thirty years of service to ensuring that justice was
done. Sending a trusted officer to notify friends far senior to
Brigadier General Buller of his intentions, he had authorized
the attendance at the court martial of Dusty, Sergeant Major
Billy Jack, and Sergeant Kiowa Cotton. All he had asked in
return for his guarantee of safe conduct was they give their
word not to take any action detrimental to the federal cause
while in Union-held territory. He had taken other precautions
to shield himself against the repercussions he anticipated might
be intended when his superior learned what he had done.

Arriving at the appointed rendezvous, although he had not
doubted this would be the case, the small Texan had concluded
McDonald intended to act in good faith. The escort for his
party was commanded by a major who had been a good friend

2. Due to having been misled by the sources from which we prepared the
manuscript for the volume of which this narrative is an "expansion," we
made it appear two other senior officers of the Army of the Confederate
States were present at the interview. A more detailed account of what was
said, not necessarily by the person to whom it was previously credited, also
regarding the two unsuccessful attempts on the life of Captain Dustine
Edward Marsden "Dusty" Fog and how he subsequently gave his evidence
at the court martial is recorded in: Part One, "The Futility of War," *The
Fastest Gun in Texas*. J. T. E.

of his father for many years. Furthermore, Colonels Sir Arnold Houghton-Rand, 2nd Dragoon Guards, and André, *Comte de Brissac*, 8th *Chasseurs à Cheval*, respectively British and French military observers, were present. Taken to the town of Mushogen, where the court martial was to take place in three days—the delay having been caused by Buller having sent word for the proceedings to be postponed until he was able to study the circumstances at first hand—the Texans were accommodated in two adjoining rooms on the first floor of the mansion used as living quarters by the officers of the Third Cavalry.

While stabling the horses, Dusty had been attacked by a supposedly drunk Corporal John Silkin. Despite the considerable difference in their respective sizes, he had not only escaped unharmed but seriously injured his assailant. The following morning, his skill with a sword and completely ambidextrous prowess had saved him from a carefully devised "accident" when he was asked by Major Montreigen—who had arrived the previous evening in Buller's retinue—to engage in a "friendly" fencing match.

Having turned in early, the small Texan was disturbed by the sound of the main entrance to his room being opened. As was often the case with men whose lives were frequently spent in hazardous conditions, he came from sleep to complete awareness without any period of dull-witted somnolence. However, apart from his left hand going to close around the butt of the Colt 1860 Army revolver he had placed beneath the pillow before retiring for the night, he lay without movement and awaited developments. Easing back the hammer with his thumb, hoping the sound would be sufficiently muffled to escape being heard, he tensed, ready to take whatever action might prove necessary and wished he was dressed in something more conducive to rapid movement than a nightshirt. Knowing he had locked the door before going to bed, he believed the need might arise. Whoever was opening it could not be entering by mistake.

"Captain Fog, sir!" a masculine voice said quietly, as a figure carrying something more bulky than a revolver, sword, or knife, stepped across the threshold from the dimly illuminated passage and closed the door. "There is no cause for alarm, sir. I mean you no harm." There was a pause, with nothing to suggest the speaker was moving farther into the room, then he continued just as quietly. "Captain Fog, are you awake, sir, please?"

"Yes," Dusty replied, keeping down the pitch of the single word to reduce the chance of betraying his exact position and, identifying the accent, wondering what had brought an Englishman to visit him in what he guessed was at least the middle of the night.

"I regret having to disturb you at such an hour, sir," the speaker went on, with a particular kind of politeness that suggested the nature of his employment. "But I must speak with you on a matter of the greatest importance to the South."

"Have you any matches?" the small Texan asked, slipping swiftly yet quietly from the bed so as to keep it between himself and his visitor.

"I have, sir."

"Then put down whatever you're carrying, take them out, and light one so I can see your face and *both* hands!"

"Very well, sir. But may I request the proviso that I cross and draw the curtains first?"

"Go ahead," Dusty authorized, glancing at the window and its open drapes. "You can start by telling me who you are."

"My name is Barnes, sir," the newcomer obliged, crossing the room to close the drapes. "Although I am here in the capacity of gentleman's personal gentleman to General Buller, I am in fact a member of the Confederate Secret Service. May I light the bedside lamp, sir, so you can see I am unarmed?"

"Go ahead and light her," the small Texan assented, the drawing of the drapes having been carried out during the explanation. "Seeing I am, I'm not 'specially worried if you are armed and I'd rather have you let me see some proof that you're what you claim to be."

"You all right, Cap'n Dusty?" Billy Jack inquired, coming through the connecting door with Kiowa on his heels, both

dressed only in shirts and breeches, but each carrying a revolver.

"I'm right enough," the small blond replied. "Couldn't you
pair sleep?"

"Kiowa snores so all fired loud it keeps him awake," the
sergeant major claimed. "Which I couldn't sleep none 'cause of
it neither."

"I figured it would be something like that," Dusty declared
dryly, assuming correctly that his companions had been taking
turns to remain awake and listening by the connecting door in
case there should be another attempt on his life. Turning his
gaze to the tall, somberly dressed, and distinguished-looking
Englishman as the bedside lamp was lit, he straightened up and
went on, "Now let's hear what you've got to say, Mr. Barnes,
and *see* some proof of it!"

"With pleasure, sir," the butler replied, although his present
status had returned him to his more usual employment as valet,
taking from his inside jacket pocket and unfolding a sheet of
paper. "My commission, sir. Perhaps Mr. Logan Huntspill of
Pine Bluff, or Jabez Wexler of Little Rock, may have shown
you the same."

"It looks real enough," Dusty admitted, after having examined the document identifying, "the bearer, Thaddeus
Barnes" and instructing all officers in the Confederate Army
and Navy to render him any assistance requested. Although he
had met the first man named and knew of the second as another
spy for the South,[3] he gave no indication of this. Instead, feeling
foolish at conducting such a conversation clad as he was, he
tossed the Colt onto the bed and continued while donning his
breeches, "But the Yankees could have come across one of
these. Which being, they'd do just as good at making a copy for
using to flimflam us Johnny Rebs with."

"I can't deny that, sir, and I applaud your caution," the

3. Meetings which Logan Huntspill and Jabez Wexler had with Captain
Dustine Edward Marsden "Dusty" Fog are recorded in: Part One, "The
Scout," *Under the Stars and Bars* and *Kill Dusty Fog!* J. T. E.

Englishman answered. "Nor, beyond hoping you will accept my *bona fides,* can I offer further proof. However, I trust you will hear me out and allow me to tell you what has brought me here to disturb you at this hour of the night."

"Sit down and tell ahead," the small Texan authorized.

"I would prefer to stand, sir," Barnes refused, with the quiet dignity that came so naturally to him. "In the first place, though, the man Silkin was not drunk and trying to avenge his comrades killed by yourself and your men during the attack on the Mushogen Bridge. He had been instructed to do so and given the excuse by Sergeant Major Packard."

"I didn't think he was smart enough to come up with a play like that on his lonesome," Dusty drawled, sitting on the bed and waving the other Texans to take chairs.

"General Buller did not know it was to happen, although he expressed his satisfaction on learning the instructions were given," the Englishman went on, studying the young captain and drawing favorable conclusions which, nevertheless, made him regret what he was intending to do. "But he did know that, in the event of Silkin failing, Major Montreigen meant to kill you by what would appear an accident."

"I sort of figured the button didn't come off the point of his *épée* by chance," Dusty asserted.

"There may be other attempts, sir," Barnes warned. "The general is bound and determined to have that young lieutenant found guilty and believes only the evidence you gentlemen can give stands between himself achieving this."

"Like sending a feller to get me to do something that would compromise me in the eyes of the Yankees before the court martial?" Dusty hinted.

"I could wish my mission was no more than that, sir," the Englishman said somberly, losing none of his high opinion as a result of the further evidence of the *big* young Texan's acumen. "But, and I can give you no assurance other than my word that I am speaking the truth, it is something of far greater import."

"Sounds bad!" Dusty breathed, after having been told of the discovery made by David Aaranovitch and the use to which it was to be put under Buller's orders. "Only I can't see either General Grant or General Sherman, much less President Lincoln happen Uncle Devil's called it right about the kind of man he is, allowing a thing like that to be turned loose on us. Apart from anything else, they'd figure like that Duke of Wellington of yours said when he was offered something similar to use against the French, 'Two can play that game.' Which, I've always been told, the winning side in a war usually figures it stands to lose more than it gains by changing the rules."

"True, sir, very true," the Englishman conceded, impressed by the surprising breadth of the youthful captain's knowledge. "However, as he has maintained most effective secrecy where his own people are concerned, General Buller will already have used the liquid and presented them with a *fait accompli.*"

"Do this here 'fait—whatever' mean what I conclude it do, Cap'n Dusty?" Billy Jack inquired. "Sort of like saying, 'I've done the son of a bitch and it's too late to stop me.'"

"That is what it means," Barnes supplied, before the small Texan could speak. "However, the ramifications go much farther than what might easily strike a crippling blow against you and your comrades-in-arms here in Arkansas. After he has demonstrated its potency in the field, he is going to inform the British and foreign military observers who are present that he will sell the formula to whichever nation is willing to pay the highest price. I don't believe I need tell you what *that* could mean, sir?"

"Every country would be after it," Dusty replied, the question having been directed to him. "And those who missed out when it's sold will set their scientists and chemists to working all out at finding something along the same lines as well as ways to counter it." He paused, studying the impassive features of his visitor for a few seconds, then went on, "And I'm starting to get a notion of why you've come to see me!"

"Yes, sir," Barnes said quietly, his voice never changing its politely unemotional timbre despite his feelings over what he must do. His instincts suggested the small Texan had been raised to a code of honor equal to that of the best type of

English gentleman he had served. Possessing a high standard of
ethics himself, he was not enamored of what he was about to
say. "As I have been unable to make an opportunity while
coming here, I want you to destroy the liquid before it can be
taken to a place where it will be beyond our reach."

"God damn it, man!" Dusty snapped, coming to his feet, and
such was the sheer strength of his personality, he no longer
appeared small. Instead, he gave the impression of being the
largest man in the room. "I'm here on parole. Do you know
what you're asking of me?"

"Only too well, sir," Barnes replied, meeting the cold stare of
the gray eyes without flinching. "I'm asking you to break your
word and take action which, in one respect, might be construed
as detrimental to the interests of the Union cause. And I assure
you, sir, I am fully cognizant with what doing so would mean
to a *gentleman* like yourself. Please accept that I would never
make such a request if there was *any* other way I could achieve
the destruction. I have the means, but was not granted an opportunity to use them while traveling and I lack the requisite
abilities to do so in the prevailing conditions."

Glancing at the small leather case indicated by the Englishman and which had been left near the door while the drapes
were being closed, Dusty sucked in a deep breath. He found
himself faced with the most demanding and difficult decision of
his young life. While he appreciated the extreme gravity of the
situation, including how a successful demonstration of the liquid's potential as a weapon might lead to its adoption and use
by other nations, he had been raised in the exacting code of
honor of the South. One thing in particular had always been
stressed throughout his upbringing, that a man's word was his
bond. Against that, despite his youth, he had a sense of humanity which revolted against the idea of anybody—not just himself and his comrades-in-arms—being subjected to such a bar-
baric and horrific form of weapon.

It was a conflict of interests capable of taxing a person of
greater age and experience than the small Texan.

"Cap'n Dusty," Billy Jack said, after having glanced at and

received a nod of concurrence from the Indian-dark sergeant. "By all accounts and what's said about us frequent, Kiowa 'n' me ain't no ways gentlemen. Which being, seeing's how we float our stick along of you in reckoning this gent's telled us truthful, you give us the word and we'll go 'tend to what *has* to be done."

"No!" the small Texan replied, stiffening and his face setting in hard lines. "It's for *me* to do."

"It's not a one-man chore, Cap'n!" Kiowa claimed.

"I know," Dusty replied. "But I can't ask you to come with me. If we're caught, it'll be a hang-rope and not a prison camp for what we were trying to do."

"There's them's reckon you're like to wind up dead one way or another, not all of 'em quick 'n' clean, should you wind up in one of them prison camps run by that Yankee General Smethurst,"[4] Kiowa commented. "And seeing's how you fetched us here with you, I druther face a hang-rope than going back to tell Ole Devil and the rest of the boys in Company C we'd come home without you."

"What they'd do to us," the sergeant major supplemented dolefully, "hanging'd be quicker 'n' more merciful-like."

"All right, damn it!" the small Texan exclaimed, looking from one noncom to the other and back. Making an effort to conceal his feeling of deep gratitude, knowing to display it would embarrass them, he forced his voice to stay even as he continued, "Why shouldn't I have you pair of useless loafers along to share the hanging with me?"

"What I've allus took to about you, Cap'n Dusty," Billy Jack announced, speaking with such miserable conviction he might have resigned himself to the inevitability of the mission failing, capture, and execution, "and that's how you're allus looking

4. Suggestions of the way in which those Union prisoner of war camps under the command of Brigadier General Lawrence Smethurst were run can be found in: *To Arms! To Arms! in Dixie!* and *Set A-Foot.* How he met his end is told in: *The Hooded Riders.* J. T. E.

for ways to do good by Kiowa 'n' me. It'll be a honor to get
hanged in such company."

"Likely," the small Texan replied, then turned his attention
to the Englishman. "All right, Mr. Barnes, let's see what you've
got in that case and tell us everything you can that will help us
get rid of that damned liquid."

"Lastly, sir, I would like to thank you on behalf of humanity," the butler said, at the conclusion of a very thorough explanation. "And I give you my word that, my duty to my country
notwithstanding, I will never mention the liquid once it has
been destroyed to *anyone* not now present in this room."[5]

5. Although we have found no confirmation, based upon the identity of the
"unsatisfactory" employer, we suspect Thaddeus Barnes had been placed in
the Confederate States' Secret Service by its counterpart in Great Britain.
This may have been done with the sanction of the British government.
Various other adverse activities led to the "Alabama" Arbitration Tribunal
after the war. Despite the alleged parting of their ways, in the as yet unpub-
lished memoirs of Major General Sir Patrick Reeder, K. C. B., V. C., M. C.
and Bar, *On Remittance,* there are several references to a Thaddeus Barnes
being valet to his father long after 1861 and mentions of them having
played the "Great Game" together during their association. J. T. E.

15

Ole Devil Will Understand

"There's one good thing, way we're going at this," Sergeant Major Billy Jack asserted in a whisper, as he and his two companions emerged from the Mushogen River to stand among a clump of bushes and study the camp on the northern bank. "We'll likely to get us 'poo-monia' and die of it afore they can hang us when they catch us doing what we've come for."

"Which you figure they will do?" Captain Dustine Edward Marsden ("Dusty") Fog announced rather than inquired.

"Certain sure to, with me along," the lanky sergeant major asserted, with what appeared to be lugubrious satisfaction. "Comes of me busting up a whole box full of mirrors in a medicine show wagon when I was a button. At seven years' bad luck apiece, I've still got me a whole slew of time to go afore I've throwed the hex."

"Ain't *everything* going to go bad, though," Sergeant Kiowa Cotton claimed. "I've been figuring on taking me a bath for a fair spell now. Which, doing it this way, I've got my clothes washed to boot."

"Put that way, it looks like some good's going to come out of this after all," the small Texan drawled, starting to remove the waterproof tarpaulin covering from the object he was carrying. "Get that thing out, Billy Jack, so's we can head over and fix it to have ourselves hung."

Before they began to obey, the noncoms exchanged brief glances and nods of approval. As each had anticipated, now the time for action was at hand, their young commanding officer had shaken off the preoccupation which had afflicted him for several hours. They had known its cause and respected him all the more for having made what they realized, although neither could fully comprehend just how great an effort of will was required, must have been a very difficult decision.

In later years, Dusty was to say the hours since the visit he had received from Thaddeus Barnes were the most miserable he ever experienced.

After supplying all the information he had acquired about the camp, displaying a sound knowledge of what was needed to help carry out the assignment, the butler had opened the leather case and shown the Texans what they would need to use to destroy the deadly liquid. He had also suggested a means by which they could leave the house. Saying he would try to obtain horses, he was assured that Kiowa was better able to attend to this aspect. However, while a plan of campaign was decided upon, the hour was too late—or rather too early in the morning—for it to be put into effect before daybreak. This, Barnes had claimed, posed no problem. Work had begun to erect a pontoon bridge across the Mushogen River, but a shortage of materials and trained workers for a task of such magnitude ensured it progressed slowly. As yet, the temporary crossing was not considered safe for use by anything other than the lightest traffic. Having such great hopes for it, Brigadier General Moses J. Buller would not entrust the two wagons loaded with the liquid already manufactured and materials required for producing more until satisfied the crossing could be made without danger.

After the butler had left the room, locking the door with the device he had used to open it, Dusty had spent a restless time until reveille. Nor had his feelings been improved by the kindness and friendliness which the officers of the Third United States Cavalry had displayed. Despite telling himself that men of their caliber would not approve of such a hideous means of waging war and might even be willing to help prevent its use, he was deeply troubled by the thought of breaking his word of honor. Nor were his pangs of conscience lessened by knowing the destruction of the vile liquid would cause a delay in which news of its discovery could be conveyed to President Abraham Lincoln and cause further developments along that line to at least be postponed. It was not even more than a slight relief to think that, should David Aaranovitch die as a result of the destruction, the world would be saved from his discovery, as he had not divulged the formula even to his employer.

Only by exerting a considerable effort of will had the small Texan contrived to conceal his despondency while in the company of the Yankee officers. Nor had he been helped in this by the evidence of their determination to prevent further incidents which might place him in jeopardy. However, nothing untoward had happened. Nor, despite Buller having been in Mushogen engaged in a lengthy conference with Colonel Iain McDonald and a representative of the Adjutant General's Department, had they met. Before he turned in for the night, he had learned Buller suggested the charges against First Lieutenant Kirby Cogshill be dropped. Stating that to do so would not be in accordance with regulations, the colonel had refused. Unless the trial took place now the preliminaries were commenced, he had claimed with the support of the legal expert that the young officer would always have the stigma of doubt, which could prove detrimental to his future advancement in the army. Although clearly anything except pleased by this decision, the general had yielded and said the court martial would take place as arranged.

Coming to join the Texans at the appointed time, Barnes had said the mission must take place that night. Buller had been informed that the bridge had been tested and was capable of taking the weight of his two wagons. Wanting to put his property in a place safe from prying eyes and have production of the liquid commenced as quickly as possible, he had dispatched a message ordering it to be brought across and sent on its way to his headquarters at daybreak. While it was unlikely that Second Lieutenant Robert Cryer would set off that early, the butler had said, the context of the instructions was such that he would not delay to any great extent once daylight had come.

Although the butler had offered to obtain civilian clothing during the day, or try to produce federal uniforms, Dusty had declined in each case. Even wearing their own uniforms, due to the conditions of their presence in the area, the task upon which he and his men intended to engage would be classed as espionage. Therefore, unless they were killed outright, retaining their own clothing offered two advantages. First, he could try to save the two noncoms by claiming they had no choice other than accompanying him as he had ordered them to do. Secondly, being the kind of man he was, Colonel McDonald would insist upon learning why an officer of the Confederate Army had broken parole. Presented with the facts, including how Buller had been an active participant in a plot to assassinate President Abraham Lincoln and intended to offer the formula for the liquid to other countries, he would ensure the Department of War in Washington heard of it. Furthermore, unless the small Texan misjudged the colonel's character, he would send a warning of the threat it posed to General Jackson Baines ("Ole Devil") Hardin. In which case, at least part of the assignment would have been achieved.

Leaving the mansion undetected by the route Barnes used to obtain access on both occasions, the party were wearing the sidearms that had not been taken from them, and were carrying the means of destruction that Barnes had prepared suitably for its delivery. Once outside, Kiowa had justified the confidence of his superior by collecting four horses and their saddles from the picket lines of the Third Cavalry's enlisted men. Thereafter, the journey to the bridge had passed uneventfully. Although the butler had proved a competent rider, admitting his skills lay in other directions than making an undetected approach to a hostile camp, he had taken the duty of keeping the animals quiet in a small patch of woodland on the southern bank a short distance upstream of their destination.

Being aware of the necessity to leave no traces of their visit and wanting to avoid killing if possible, as was demanded by his conscience under the circumstances, Dusty and his noncoms had left their firearms in Barnes's care. Advancing on foot, they had swum across the river near the edge of the encampment and were ready to continue their assignment.

Regardless of the remarks they had been making, the Texans were aware of how the uncomfortable condition of their clothing could be to their advantage. The majority of the Yankees were already turned in for the night in the lines of tents, but there were sentries posted. While the moon was on the wane, it still gave sufficient light to put their scheme in jeopardy if it had allowed the lighter color of their uniforms to be seen. However, they were bareheaded, and being wet, the material was given a darker hue which could pass as Union blue.

Having had considerable experience in such matters, based upon the excellent information received from Barnes regarding the layout and routine of the camp, Dusty and his men had settled upon the way they believed offered the best chance of reaching their destination. One of the factors in their decision was having been told by the butler that the bushes in which they stood were used as a latrine by the occupants of the camp. Therefore, it was an area from which a sentry would be accustomed to seeing men appear, and he would be less likely to feel suspicious than if an approach was made from some other point on the perimeter.

"Let's go get her done, boys!" Dusty said quietly, as two square wooden boxes were exposed by the removal of the waterproof coverings. "Unless they've been moved, Buller's wagons are off on their own a mite, with his own men guarding them."

"Shouldn't go causing us no sweat, nor worrying, happen they're no better'n that other bunch of New Hampstead Volunteers we run up against," Billy Jack declared, then realized such a display of optimism was not in keeping with his assumed attitude toward life. "Less'n we fall over something and make so much noise they wakes up and catches us, that is."

"Happen *we* do," the small Texan growled, simulating exasperation, "so help me, I'm going to ask them to let me kick the box out from under you, comes our hanging."

"You won't get the chance," the sergeant major asserted. "Happen I don't die of the 'pooh-monia' first, I'll likely fall off 'n' bust my neck going up the steps to the scaffold."

"Why, sure," Dusty drawled, having learned it was almost impossible to get the better of his lanky subordinate in such exchanges. "I'll head out there and get shot first. Mind you don't keep them waiting to do it to you."

"That boy's being put through all hell doing this, *amigo*," Kiowa commented, as the small Texan set off across the open ground carrying one of the boxes.

"Comes of being born and raised a gentleman," Billy Jack replied, with none of his false pessimism or derision in his voice. "Going again' his given word don't come easy to a *man* like Cap'n Dusty, young as he is."

"Ole Devil will understand when he hears," the Indian-dark sergeant claimed, reaching behind his neck to loosen the knife concealed in its sheath beneath the collar of his tunic. "And nobody else'd best mean-mouth Cap'n Dusty for doing it where I can hear 'em."

Oblivious of the sentiments uttered by his companions, Dusty walked toward the collection of unhitched wagons awaiting the bridge being made strong enough to take their weight. While apparently unconcerned, as a Yankee would be when returning from using the bushes as a latrine, he was tense and alert. Not far away, unauthorized cigarettes glowing redly, a couple of sentries stood talking at the end of the bridge. How-

ver, he reached the shelter of the vehicles without either pay-
ng the slightest attention to him. Halting in the shadows, he
vaited with bated breath as Kiowa followed in a similar fash-
on. Once again, the crossing of the open ground went unchal-
enged.

Allowing a couple of minutes to elapse, Billy Jack emerged
rom concealment carrying the second box. Before he had
aken his tenth step, one of the sentries spoke urgently to the
ther and both tossed their cigarettes into the river.

For a moment, which seemed far longer to the sergeant ma-
or and his watching companions, it seemed the third appear-
nce in so short a time had aroused the suspicions of the first
oldier. However, knowing to do otherwise would confirm a
upposition of something being amiss, he continued with his
teady and apparently disinterested advance. He was a poker
layer of note, and bluff was a prime requisite of that game, but
e was aware he had never played for such high stakes. The
uccess of the mission and the lives of his companions were
anging in the balance. Their fate and his own depended en-
irely upon his ability to convince the Yankees that he, too, was
rom the camp and had been engaged in the usual harmless
ursuit among the bushes.

Shouldering his rifle, instead of turning it into a position of
eadiness with the barrel pointed in the direction of the lanky
ergeant major, the speaker swung and marched briskly away
long the bank of the river. Adopting a more militaristic atti-
ude, the second sentry also betrayed no interest whatsoever in
illy Jack or the other Texans. Before the sergeant major could
ejoin his companions, the reason for the change in the pair's
ehavior became obvious. Striding from the tent line a stocky
nd middle-sized figure, whose dress and armament indicated
e served in the New Hampstead Volunteers and was doing
uty as officer of the day, made for the bridge.

"Goddamned Yankee officer-boy!" Billy Jack breathed, as he
ame up to Dusty and Kiowa. "He scared me like to make me
iss my breeches!"

"You saw him too, huh?" the small Texan inquired, sounding surprised.

"Well, yes," Billy Jack replied. "I could just about reckon you might say I saw the son of a bitch."

"*Bueno!*" Dusty said, in the fashion of one conveying praise. "I take to a man's stays alert. Let's get going afore he comes this way."

Apart from keeping to the shadows as much as possible and refraining from talking, the Texans' behavior seemed better suited to walking through a camp occupied by their own people than that of the enemy. They were aware that to skulk along would make their intentions obvious, while the method of progress they were employing suggested they had a right to be there. However, due to a number of vehicles having arrived since Barnes left for Mushogen, they found difficulty in following his directions and were compelled to check the insignia on the canopies to identify the pair they sought.

"You men!" a voice called, as the Texans had located the wagons. "What are you doing out here?"

Turning their heads and halting, Dusty and his companions saw the fancily uniformed officer of the day approaching. Reaching toward the hilt of the knife concealed by the collar of his tunic, Kiowa glanced at but received a prohibitive shake of the head from the small Texan. However, instead of lowering his hand, he changed the movements to rub at the back of his neck as if it was sore or aching.

"Well!" Second Lieutenant Robert Cryer snapped, looking the trio over as he came to a halt before them. "I asked you a question!"

"Sure you did, sir," Dusty answered, adopting what he hoped would pass as an Irish brogue. "And it's down by the mess tent we've been to catch some rats."

"*Rats?*" Cryer repeated, his voice indicative of puzzlement rather than suspicion.

"Rats it is, sir," the small Texan declared, indicating Billy Jack with the box he was carrying and holding it forward. "Sure and isn't it the best rat-killing Irish terrier in the world

he O'Reilly here is having to take care of 'em for our amusement. Would you like to see the little devils, sir?"

"No!" the lieutenant refused, stepping backward a pace.
"And you're not to disturb the camp by doing it tonight!"

"Sir and such wasn't never our intentions, sir," Dusty replied. "'Tis for the enjoyment of me and the other boys we've
done the catching and they're not expecting nothing from us
afore the morning's morning."

Eager to get to his bed now he had carried out the rounds
that were required of the officer of the day, Cryer gave not a
thought to the way in which the diminutive "enlisted man" was
doing all the talking, regardless of the other two bearing the
chevrons of senior noncoms on their sleeves. At that moment,
the benefit of the still wet clothing was manifesting itself. Dusty
had removed the gold bars from his collar, and, never of an
observant nature, the lieutenant failed to notice the "chicken
guts" insignia above the cuffs of his jacket. Nor, lacking imagi-
nation, did it occur to him that three men walking so openly in
a Union Army's camp were actually Confederate soldiers. Returning the salutes they gave in a casual fashion, he walked
away without so much as a backward glance.

"Whooee!" Billy Jack breathed, glancing to where Kiowa
was taking the hand from the back of his neck. "There goes a
jasper who'll never know how close he come to being made
wolf bait."

"Yeah," agreed the Indian-dark sergeant, looking first at the
speaker, then to the small Texan. "And I thought *you* could
run a bluff at poker, Billy Jack. But don't you *never* ask me to
sit in on a game with you, Cap'n Dusty."

"I'll mind it," the young captain promised. "But would you
have figured out what we really are in his place?"

"Likely not," Kiowa conceded.

"Well, we've found what we come after," Dusty stated, making sure Cryer had gone from view. "I don't see the guards put
on them, though."

"Or me," the sergeant declared, after studying the two vehicles. "Could be inside, maybe."

"We'll likely find that's where they are," Billy Jack claimed, with his usual pretense at pessimism. "Let's go look and make fools of ourselves."

Scanning their surroundings with great care, the Texans resumed their advance. They were surprised and pleased on reaching the wagons to have escaped being challenged and to receive an indication that they were incorrect in their assumption. As the canopies were secured, it struck them as unlikely the guards would be inside. Yet, from what they had been told by Barnes, they had expected a watch to be kept. What they and he had failed to take into account was the type of men with whom they were dealing.

Having ambitions toward a career in local politics, Cryer was ever ready to curry favor with men who might one day be in a position to give him their votes. Therefore, when left in command, he had not tried to enforce the instructions given by his superior. Nor were the enlisted men of the Volunteers any more prone to attend to their duties voluntarily. The only reason the lieutenant had come across the Texans was that, the major commanding the camp having decided to make the most of him before he departed in the morning, he was assigned to be officer of the day.

Putting down his box as he and his companions reached the nearer wagon, Billy Jack studied the lashings of its canopy. Something of a master of handling ropes, he had promised to do all he could to unfasten and then retie in the same fashion whatever kind of knots were used. Giving a sniff of disdain at what his eyes and questing fingers discovered, he found not the slightest difficulty in carrying out the first part of his task.

As soon as a sufficient gap was made, Dusty climbed into the wagon and Kiowa closed the flaps behind him. Opening the box, he felt for and removed a box of matches and a candle. Using one of the former to light the latter, he examined the interior with the aid of its small glow. His main attention was given to two large carboys in protective coverings standing at the front. Climbing over the other items, all of which had been packed carefully to prevent any chance of their sliding against and breaking the containers of the lethal liquid, he placed the box between their wicker-work covers. Then he reached inside.

The box contained a combined explosive and incendiary device which could be detonated by a clockwork mechanism.

Carrying out the instructions received from the butler, the small Texan set the timing mechanism to perform its function at the end of four hours. By doing so, he hoped to cause the destruction with the wagons well clear of the camp and reduce loss of life as far as possible. Waiting until he heard the gentle ticking, he retreated to the back of the wagon and, blowing out the candle, emerged.

"The other 'n's ready for you, Cap'n Dusty," Billy Jack informed. "I'll fasten this the exact same way it was while you're 'tending to it!"

An hour later, the Texans rejoined Barnes.

"We did it," Dusty announced, although the butler had made no request to be told. "Now it all depends on those infernal devices you gave us."

"You can rely upon them to function properly, sir," Barnes claimed with complete confidence, and his austere features came as close to smiling as the Texans had ever seen. "And may I say that I will derive not a little pleasure from seeing my employer's face when he hears his precious liquid is gone. In my opinion, while a general officer, he is *not* a gentleman."

"Never yet met a Yankee who was," Billy Jack lied, for there were several—including Colonel Iain McDonald—he regarded in such a light. "Thing sticks in my craw, though, is that son of a bitch who made the goddamned stuff's still around to whomp up some more of it."

"Not for long," the butler replied, and although his expression and tone never changed, there was something in his demeanor that caused the Texans—experienced in such matters—to conclude he was a man whose path it would be exceedingly dangerous to cross. "Mr. Aaranovitch is no horseman and will, I anticipate, be riding on one of the wagons. However, should this not be the case, or he survives the conflagration, I will ensure he is not able to repeat his efforts. I hope, nevertheless, the need does not arise. If he dies after eating a meal I have prepared, it may arouse adverse comment with respect to the quality of my cooking."

16

I'll Show You How to Kill Fog

"It's not guilty!" Major Saul Montreigen reported without any preliminaries, wondering whether the news he and Sergeant Major Alden Packard had brought was already known to his glowering and obviously furious superior. "The court preferred Fog's story to that of our friend here, but he came out of it *just* clear of being charged with perjury."

"I don't give a shit what the verdict was, or how *he* came out of it!" Brigadier General Moses J. Buller raged, without so much as a glance at the scowling and very worried noncom. "All the goddamned liquid gas has *gone!*"

It was eleven o'clock on the day of the court martial of First Lieutenant Kirby Cogshill.

Commencing promptly at nine o'clock, after the charges had been read, the prosecutor had tried to obtain a postponement because one of his witnesses was not available. On learning how Corporal John Silkin had sustained the injury which prevented his appearing before them, the officers forming the court had declined to delay the proceedings. Sensing from the composition of the court that its members were unlikely to be concerned with the possibility of arousing Buller's wrath, Packard had toned down his story until it appeared he was merely misled by the behavior of the young lieutenant and had, in fact, based his complaint upon what he was told by the absent corporal. Having heard the evidence given by Captain Dustine Edward Marsden ("Dusty") Fog and his two men, the court had not even bothered to leave their places before announcing a verdict of not guilty.

At the suggestion of the adviser from the Adjutant General's Department, the general had not attended the court. Instead, while waiting in his suite at the best hotel in Mushogen, he had received the news that put him in the state of vile temper he had displayed to his two subordinates on their arrival.

"Gone?" Montreigen repeated. "How did it go?"

"How the mother-something hell do I *know*?" Buller snarled. "The wagons blew up on their way here!"

"Blew up?" the major queried.

"That's what I said!" the general bawled. "And don't ask me how it happened!"

"Aaranovitch knows how to make some more," Montreigen pointed out.

"Aaranovitch was riding on one of the goddamned mother-something wagons!" Buller answered savagely. "Why the hell didn't I *make* him give me the formula?" Then he looked at the other officer with mingled suspicion and hope, going on in a somewhat less hostile fashion, "You were with him all the time he was working on the son of a bitch. Surely you know how he made it, or at least what he used?"

"Not me," Montreigen lied, but with such vehemence and apparent disappointment he might have been speaking the truth. While the chemist had not told him any more than was known by the general, he had had a man with similar knowledge acquire the information unbeknown to the producer of the liquid gas. "He wouldn't let anybody in the kitchen when he was working on it. Hell, I tried, but all he did was stand around and do nothing until I left."

"God rot his guts!" Buller snarled. "Didn't you even have the sense to make a list of the things he bought to mix it?"

"I tried doing it," the major admitted truthfully, the failure having caused him to make use of a second chemist without disclosing anything of the purpose of the various items. "But he always ordered everything himself, and the containers it came in were marked in a way only he knew."

"Somebody *had* to know, though!" the general said, more to himself than his subordinates. "I can find them and get in touch with whoever it was he got his gear from and then I'll easy enough find another chemist to make me some more."

"There might be an even easier way," Montreigen suggested, having hoped such a possible solution had not occurred to his superior. "Aaranovitch had got real cozy and lovie-dovie with Cryer, so maybe he was told the formula."

"He took it to hell with him if he was!" Buller asserted. "The idle, useless bastard was riding on the wagon with Aaranovitch!"

"Is there a chance of finding something about it from the wagons?" the major inquired, although the last thing he wanted as things had turned out was an answer in the affirmative.

"Not a single goddamned part of a hope!" the general replied bitterly. "Aaranovitch told me the goddamned stuff was highly inflammable and the son of a bitch was all of that. The man who brought me the news said both wagons were burned down almost to the axles, and except for the bodies that were blown off, everything else was gone."

"Where did it happen?" Montreigen wanted to know, Packard having concluded the best thing he could do was remain silent and hope his failure to procure a verdict of guilty against Cogshill would be overlooked in the face of this latest disaster.

"At a hollow where the trail runs through those woods about three miles out of town. That and the trees all round must have stopped the explosion being heard."

"Who told you about it?"

"The men I sent to find out why the wagons hadn't got here," Buller answered. "Everything was over when they got there. But from what they said, I reckon that useless bastard Cryer didn't get moving until long after I said for him to be on his way here." Pausing to suck in a long breath, such was the depth of his emotion, he continued, "From what they heard, the wagons were rolling along when there was a couple of bangs and first one, then the other son of a bitch went up in a sheet of flames. Those of the escort who weren't blown up got thrown off their horses when it happened and still hadn't been able to either get back to the bridge or come here!"

"You say there were a couple of bangs *before* the fires started?" Montreigen queried. "One in *each* wagon?"

"Of course it was one in *each* wagon!" Buller growled, having no intention of admitting he had not thought to raise the point when hearing the news. "That's why they *both* went up in flames."

"How?" the major inquired.

"How?" the general snarled. "Some of those goddamned chemicals must have got knocked and did it is *how*!"

"They've been brought a long way and not handled overgently on occasion," Montreigen reminded his superior. "So why did they suddenly go off and not just *one* wagon, but *both* almost at the same time?"

"What the hell are you getting at?"

"I'm always suspicious of coincidences, particularly when they happen so inconveniently."

"Are you saying somebody blew them up deliberately?"

"Yes!"

"Who could have done it?"

"How about the Rebs?" Montreigen suggested.

"Rebs!" Buller snorted disdainfully. "Nobody except—hell, only you and me are left who know. So how would the Rebs have found out?"

"They've got some pretty good spies all through the North," the major supplied. "In fact, thinking about what happened to Flannery, I've been asking around ever since we left Washington. From what I've heard, one of the best they have is a slender, but well-built, real good-looking girl called Belle Boyd."

"Belle Boyd?" Buller gasped, the description arousing a disturbing thought.

"They call her the Rebel Spy, she's so good," Montreigen elaborated. "According to what I've heard, she can fight barehanded like a sack filled with starving bobcats and is better than fair at that French kick-boxing they call 'savate,' and going by what you said about that fight at Wigg's, the 'French-Canadian' girl showed she was pretty handy at it."

"She *was*!" the general conceded vehemently. "But—!"

"She'd grown up among them and could make herself sound like a high-toned rich *Creole*," the major continued remorselessly. "Which's why she wouldn't talk French to *me*, in case I'd have known for sure she wasn't from Canada."

"Nobody knew what I'd got Aaranovitch doing!" Buller protested.

"There was enough around who knew *something* was going on," Montreigen countered. "And even if it had only been trying to find out a new way of preserving food like we said, those goddamned Rebs would be even keener than our own folks to learn what was doing. The more important they thought it might be, the more likely they'd be to use the Rebel Spy to get to know. Then, having found out, you can bet everything you've got they'd be bound and determined to stop you from proving how effective that liquid gas could be."

"But she ran out the night she saw it!" the general objected, trying to convince himself he had not been made a fool of by the girl introduced to him as Françoise.

"That could be because she'd had to kill Flannery when he caught her going out to tell another of their spies what she'd learned," the major guessed, drawing a similarly accurate conclusion with regards to the reason for the comment. "And there was the time *you* stayed on in Washington trying to set up that deal with Mary Wilkinson. That would have let them get word to Ole Devil Hardin, so he could stop you from turning the gas loose on his men."

"Hardin?"

"He's the Reb general who'd be affected first by it."

"I know that!" Buller snorted. "But how the hell did he get it done?"

"Doesn't it strike you as strange that Hardin would take all the trouble he did just to save the neck of a Yankee luff?" Montreigen inquired, feeling sure his uncouth and unprincipled superior would have neither a conception of nor belief in the Southron code of honor. "And can you think of a better way to have three of his men, those three in particular, allowed into our territory?"

"It can't have been them!" the general protested. "They were kept at McDonald's place all the time."

"And would be able to come and go as they pleased, because he trusted them to keep their word," the major replied. "From all I've heard about Fog and his men, they could have sneaked out, got horses, gone to the camp on the Mushogen River, put some kind of infernal devices set off by time mechanisms, and been back without leaving a trace of it, before morning."

"By God!" Buller thundered, face reddening with rage. "I'll go and have all three of those bastards taken and—!"

"That's not the way to deal with it!" Montreigen warned, moving to block the impending departure of his superior. "You haven't any proof that they did it!"

"Just let me have them," the general spat out, seeming to be on the point of grabbing and throwing aside the other officer. "And I'll soon enough have the goddamned truth out of their son-of-a-bitching hides!"

"McDonald will want to know why you've taken them before you can do it," Montreigen pointed out, showing no sign of flinching before the other's wrath. "And, if you give him the truth—!"

"God damn it, I outrank the Scotch bastard!" Buller thundered, having halted, his voice filled with a close to petulant fury. "He'll have to take whatever reason I give him!"

"Unless it's the truth, you'll need a stronger story than I can think up for such action!" the major contradicted. "Don't forget, his career would be on the line seeing as how it was him insisted on allowing them to come here. He's smart enough to figure there was something out of the ordinary in those wagons, from the way they burned so violently, even without the Rebs believing their cargo was worth taking such trouble to get rid of it. What's more, Fog is Hardin's nephew and he'll do anything he can, even to letting McDonald know why the young bastard was sent. He could even get word of it to Washington and that'll do what you've been trying to avoid. Even if the general staff decided to follow up on Aaranovitch's work, they'll make good and sure you don't have a chance to sell the formula to other countries."

"Are you saying I've got to sit back and let that short-grown peckerwood bastard get away with what he's done?" Buller demanded.

"No," Montreigen replied. "If you're game to try it, I'll show you how to kill Fog in a way that won't let Hardin know you suspect what he was up to, and the reputation he's built up, what with capturing Cussing Culver and all, you could even come out of it with some favor."

"If that's what you reckon," the general growled, thinking of how his predecessor in command of the Army of Arkansas had been captured by the young Texan, and of other incidents attributed to the same source. "You tell me how I can kill him and I'll show you I'm game enough to try it!"

"General Buller wants me to state that he has no knowledge of handling a sword," Major Montreigen announced. "He wishes to fight with pistols."

"That is to the satisfaction of our principal!" replied Colonel Baron Ludwig von Dettmer, Prussian military observer who, along with Colonel Sir Arnold Houghton-Rand, was acting as second for Captain Dusty Fog, after having asked if this was acceptable by their principal.

"Furthermore," Montreigen continued, "as we have been unable to find a pair of dueling pistols at such short notice, the general suggests each use his own Colt revolver. That will be

fair to both participants and each will have only the nipple of
the cylinder next to fall under the hammer capped. Will that be
satisfactory?"

"We accept," Houghton-Rand confirmed, having received a
nod of concurrence from the small Texan.

"Then prepare your principals' weapons, gentlemen!" instructed Colonel André, *Comte* du Brissac, acting as controller
of the duel that was about to take place in the orchard behind
the mansion used as officers' quarters by the Third Cavalry. He
concluded such behavior was acceptable by the *code duello* of
the United States of America.

"If you will take the caps from Captain Fog's revolver, Major," Houghton-Rand offered, "I will attend to that of General
Buller."

"Certainly," Montreigen replied.

"Bring me Captain Fog's revolver, Sergeant Major!" the English colonel called.

"Yo!" Billy Jack assented, removing the weapon from the
holster of his commanding officer's gunbelt, which he carried
across his left shoulder, and advancing to do as he was instructed.

Having decided the suggestions made by Montreigen would
offer him an excellent chance of taking his revenge upon the
young man he—correctly as it happened—believed responsible
for the loss of the liquid gas, Buller had put them into effect.
Going to a reception being given for Lieutenant Cogshill by the
officers of the Third Cavalry, he had pretended to be drunk and
provoked the small Texan into issuing a challenge to a duel.
With the foreign military observers present, Colonel McDonald
had been unable to prevent it from taking place. All he had
been able to do was have the affair postponed until the following morning, hoping his superior would have sobered sufficiently to call it off. This had not happened and he was compelled to let events take their course without further
interference on his part.

Although the selected venue was in the grounds of the mansion, all the officers other than those participating had been

ordered to keep clear of the area. Convention demanded that Dusty have two seconds, and wanting to avoid possible repercussions or embarrassment, he had asked the English and Prussian military observers to act for him. The same reason had caused the French colonel to be made controller and the local doctor to officiate. Serving as witnesses to report to General Jackson Baines ("Ole Devil") Hardin that all had been conducted fairly, Billy Jack and Sergeant Kiowa Cotton were present. Although the former was carrying his superior's weapon belt, they had left their own in the room they had been using. In addition to Montreigen, the general had Packard—promoted to second lieutenant in gratitude for the misguided way in which he had behaved over the death of Major Gerald Buller, or so it had been announced—acting as a second.

Exchanging the Colt 1860 Army revolver for the one he was holding, the major removed all but one of the copper percussion caps from it. Having done the same with the walnut-butted weapon he was given, Houghton-Rand passed it back. Seeing Montreigen doing so, he eased the hammer to half cock and rotated the cylinder of the bone-handled revolver until the remaining cap would be placed beneath it at the next operation of the mechanism.

Turning away after this was done, the major walked to where Buller was standing well clear of the others. Moving with a speed that implied he was not performing such a deed for the first time, he opened his tunic and extracted an almost identical revolver to the one he was holding and thrust the first back into its place. Fastening the buttons, he gave the second Colt to his superior.

"Here!" Montreigen breathed. "Don't forget what I told you!"

"I won't!" the general answered, glancing down to ensure the cylinder's nipples were all capped ready for use.

On receiving a signal from du Brissac, Dusty and Buller went to where he was standing. Each was bareheaded and had removed his tunic. Although Dusty had attended the court martial in the correct attire of an officer in the Confederate

Cavalry, he had reverted to his more usual style of uniform and had on a white shirt, riding breeches, and Hessian-leg boots.

"Is there no chance of a reconciliation, gentlemen?" the French colonel inquired formally, as the intended combatants stood, each with his revolver in the right hand and muzzle downward. When there was a negative response from both, he continued, "Then stand back to back and cock your weapons. With this done, I will say 'Commence,' and as you step off, begin to count. When I reach ten, both will turn and fire. Is that understood?"

"It is," Dusty confirmed and went to the spot indicated by du Brissac, drawing the hammer of his Colt to fully cocked as he raised it until holding it perpendicular by his right ear.

"Yes!" Buller assented a moment later, advancing to stand as instructed and adopting a similar position of readiness with his weapon.

"Commence!" the Frenchman commanded. "One! Two! Three!"

Perspiration began to form on Buller's porcine features as he stepped out the paces. Despite the advantage he possessed as a result of Montreigen's duplicity, he was nervous. While he had allowed himself far more ammunition with which to practice shooting than had been made available to the enlisted men of the New Hampstead Volunteers, he was aware that he was far from being an accomplished shot with a revolver. Nor, until that moment, had he envisaged the need for greater skill, as it had never been his intention to take a personal part in the fighting. On the other hand, youthful appearance notwithstanding, the Texan he no longer regarded as being small and insignificant in appearance had seen action several times and undoubtedly possessed far greater expertise.

"Four! Five! Six!"

Listening to the count and continuing to walk, the general decided he had only one hope of salvation.

"Seven!"

Without giving a thought to the consequences, or anything

other than saving himself from being shot, Buller put the idea into effect.

"Look out, Dusty!" Billy Jack yelled, forgetting the military honorific in the urgency of the situation.

On taking his eighth step, Buller swung around. Halting sideways to his intended target, left hand going to rest on his hip, his right lifted the Army Colt into the shoulder-high and arm's-length posture he had learned from Montreigen. Taking aim more quickly than he would have wished, as shouts of alarm and warning burst from most of the other onlookers, he squeezed on the trigger. The long-barreled weapon crashed, its bullet hissing just over Dusty's head. In his haste, the general had flinched at the last moment and missed. Snarling with rage as the recoil kick raised the Colt, apparently forgetting there was only supposed to be one chamber of the cylinder fitted with a percussion cap, he started to cock the hammer with his thumb.

At the sound of the shot, Dusty turned fast.

Seeing what Buller was doing, the small Texan knew there was not a moment to lose.

Knowing the general was not making a mistake and the revolver was fully capped, Dusty reacted to the treachery. Not for him the fancy posture of a conventional duelist. There was no time for him to adopt it, even if he had been so inclined. Instead, halting on spread-apart feet and slightly bent legs, with torso inclined forward to offer a smaller target, he brought his bone-handled Army Colt to waist height and central in respect to his body.

Such was the stance of a frontier gunfighter, used to starting in leather and drawing to hit a mark the size of the human torso in not much over a second. For all that, it was not a method conducive to excessive accuracy except at close quarters.

With his own weapon conforming to the conditions of the duel, the small Texan was aware he had only one load available to him and this one must be made to count.

17
I'll Take You First, Fog

Roaring and sending out the contents of its solitary-capped cylinder, the Colt 1860 Army revolver justified the misgivings of Brigadier General Moses J. Buller with regards to the skill of Captain Dustine Edward Marsden ("Dusty") Fog.

Flying as truly as could be hoped when directed in such a fashion, the .44 bullet took the burly Yankee officer between the eyes. On striking, it caused a reflex action, which discharged the weapon he was holding. However, the barrel was turned from its alignment and came even less close than its predecessor to achieving a hit upon the small Texan. Going over, the revolver slipping from his lifeless grasp, he was dead before his body alighted supine on the ground.

"Excuse me, gentlemen!" a coldly commanding masculine voice called, bringing an end to the startled and angry comments that were arising from the foreign military observers. The words caused them all to look to where Thaddeus Barnes was approaching through the trees of the orchard. "I am afraid

I cannot allow my former employer to bear the stigma of what he had done alone. He was put up to this base act by Major Saul Montreigen!"

Which was true enough.

Montreigen had spoken the truth when telling Belle Boyd he had operated a *salle des armes* in New Orleans before the War Between the States. It had not rated among the better-known and highly respected of such establishments in the city, but had had one special service to offer. Regardless of laws prohibiting dueling, the engagement in "affairs of honor" had continued to take place throughout the South. There had frequently been those seeking his aid who, while disinclined to incur the social stigma of refusing a challenge, were disinclined to take the risks of fair combat. In addition to giving instruction in swordsmanship and shooting, he had also given advice on survival by employing measures that went beyond the rules of the *code duello*.

Being aware of the major's unsavory past, Buller had had no hesitation before accepting his proposals for taking revenge upon Dusty Fog.

However, loyalty to a superior who was also an employer had not caused Montreigen to suggest the means of taking vengeance.

Appreciating just as much as Buller the potential for profit offered by its manufacture, the major had realized on hearing of the consignment being destroyed along with its maker that now only two people—unless one counted whoever Belle Boyd had informed of it—knew such a thing could be produced. Accepting there was nothing he could do about the Southrons, he had seen how he might cause the removal of the other participant in the knowledge. Suspecting his superior would not issue the challenge to the small Texan unless believing the result was a foredrawn conclusion, he had made his proposals, satisfied that he personally could not be the loser no matter how the duel turned out. On hearing of such a gross example of misconduct, should Buller win, Colonel McDonald's sense of honor would demand that he be brought to justice for it. What was

more, knowing that what had happened was witnessed by the
three military observers from Europe, the general staff and
leading politicians would know that the effect upon the rela-
tionship of the United States and the country each represented
would be adverse unless Buller paid for what would amount to
murder. Although an accomplice, Montreigen hoped to escape
too severe consequences by claiming he had been ordered by
Buller to help. He would almost certainly be cashiered and
dismissed from the service, but this would merely allow him to
devote more time to finding how the liquid was made.

While the fully loaded revolver had failed to produce the
promised result for the general, mainly due to his attempt to
acquire an even greater advantage, the major had been far from
disappointed by the result until hearing Barnes.

"You lying bastard!" Montreigen snarled, right hand flashing
across to bring the *épée de combat* from its sheath. "I'll make
you change your tune. Keep them all back, Packard. You're in
this too!"

Having been taken partly into the confidence of the major,
Second Lieutenant Alden Packard—as he now thought of himself—concluded that his days as even a sergeant major were
numbered. What was more, he also had reason to hate the
small Texan whom he blamed for everything that had befallen
him. Snarling a curse, he knocked open the flap of his holster,
and his right hand closed about the fancy Tiffany grips of the
Colt Model of 1855 Navy revolver he had looted from the body
of Major Gerald Buller. Knowing none of the others present
had firearms on their persons, he was confident he could acquire the acclaim Montreigen had promised the general would
accrue to the man who removed such a competent young officer
as Dusty Fog from the conflict on the Arkansas battlefront.

"Montreigen!" the small Texan shouted, allowing the inoper-
able Army Colt to slip from his grasp and starting to move
forward. "See if you have better luck than last time you tried to
kill me, you stinking hired butcher!"

"All right!" the major answered, swinging toward his chal-
lenger. "I'll take you first, Fog!"

Even as the words were being spoken, others present were preparing to intervene.

Although Sergeant Major Billy Jack and Sergeant Kiowa Cotton had obeyed their commanding officer and left their revolvers behind, neither was completely unarmed.

Having reverted to his skirtless tunic and riding breeches, after having worn full-dress uniform and accoutrements at the court martial, Dusty had been wearing his western-style rig instead of the type of weapon belt proscribed in the *Manual of Dress Regulations.* Therefore, the saber being carried suspended from the saddlehorn when he was clad in such a fashion, there was a second bone-handled Army Colt in its holster. This was readily available to the lanky sergeant major. While the Indian-dark sergeant had no firearms, he was still carrying the knife in its concealed sheath.

Moving from where they had stood slightly apart from the officials of the duel, each Texan showed a complete understanding of how the other was meaning to cope with the situation.

Extracting and thumb-cocking the Colt as he tossed aside the gunbelt, Billy Jack showed how well he could use even an unfamiliar revolver. Swinging it up and taking sight, he sent a bullet into the center of Packard's chest. Spun around as his stolen Colt was clearing its cumbersome holster, the burly "officer" fell to the ground. He made an effort to force himself onto hands and knees, then went limp and sprawled facedown again.

Despite knowing how well his superior could fight with bare hands, Kiowa was not willing, under the circumstances, to let this take place. For all his faults, Montreigen was an excellent swordsman, and his weapon gave him a decided edge over the unarmed-combat techniques learned from Tommy Okasi. With that in mind, the sergeant reached upward with his right hand. Bringing the knife from inside his collar, he swept his arm down and made a throw with all the skill at his command. Flashing through the air, the blade buried itself deep into the left breast of the major. Shock and agony distorted his swarthy face. Releasing the *épée,* his right hand went to join the left in gripping the hilt of the weapon that he sensed had struck him a mortal blow. All his strength ebbed away before he could pull it out, and crumpling like a doll from which all the stuffing had been removed, he toppled dying a few feet in front of the small young man he had tried to kill.

"I must apologize to you, Captain Fog," Thaddeus Barnes said, coming into the stable where the three Texans were saddling their horses ready for setting off to rejoin their regiment beyond the Oauchita River. Glancing around to ensure he would not be heard by anybody other than the trio, he went on, "I was aware of the plot to kill you in the duel, but I was watched over so carefully—at, I suspect, the instigation of Major Montreigen— that I was unable to warn you. However, having seen my late employer shoot, I did not doubt you would emerge victorious, and you fully justified my confidence. May I ask how Colonel McDonald responded to the news of what has happened?"

"He's written a full report to be sent to Washington and given copies to the three military correspondents, and has provided another for General Hardin," Dusty Fog replied. "He also apologized to me on behalf of the United States Army for the way Buller and his crowd behaved."

"I anticipated no less, sir," the Englishman declared. "From our first meeting, I knew him to be an officer and a gentleman." Taking an envelope from the inside breast pocket of his jacket, he darted another swift look about him before going on, "I have taken the liberty of writing and informing General Hardin of why you did what I asked of you, sir."

"Gracias," the small Texan said quietly, yet with genuine gratitude, accepting the document.

"I know how badly you feel about it, sir," Barnes asserted, with a gentleness and respect which impressed the two listening noncoms. "But, by doing so, you have rendered a service not only to the Confederate States but to all humanity in my opinion, and unless I am mistaken, General Hardin will regard it in the same light. You, sir, have done your full duty as an officer and a gentleman."

"Thank you again, Mr. Barnes," Dusty answered, holding forward his right hand.

"You know, sir," the Englishman remarked, after he and the small Texan had shaken hands, "I find your presence here not without its, shall we say, *interesting* aspects. As I understand it, you wounded Mr. Cogshill on the one previous occasion you met each other?"

"Seemed like the thing to do at the time," Dusty drawled.

"And if you meet again in action, you'll fire upon him perhaps with more lethal effect?"

"Likely."

"And yet, without your evidence, he might have been shot by order of the court martial," Barnes pointed out. "Would it have made any difference if he had died at their hands, or perhaps later at yours?"

"Not over much," Dusty admitted. "Except to his honor."

"That is true," the Englishman admitted, nodding approvingly. "Yet you have risked your life to save his and still would kill him in action should you meet again."

"Why sure," the small Texan agreed, "it makes a man think how futile war is."